Black Child
to
Black Woman

An African-American Woman Coming-of-Age Story

Cheryl Denise Bannerman

2ND Edition

Print format: ISBN 978-1-7353352-0-9

Electronic format: ISBN 978-1-7353352-1-6

Audio format: Retail ISBN: 9781094226088 and

Library ISBN: 9781094226088

To those who:

Doubted me
Judged me
Could not be flexible
Mocked me
Took advantage of me
Thought I couldn't
Put me down
Abandoned me
Refused to understand me
or took me for granted…

This is for you.

Content

Prologue

In a Letter to My Daughter, Maya Angelou writes, "I am convinced that most people do not grow up...We marry and dare to have children and call that growing up. I think what we do is mostly grow old. We carry accumulation of years in our bodies, and on our faces, but generally our real selves, the children inside, are innocent and shy as magnolias."

I was slowly becoming a woman, a responsible adult, and someone my parents could continue to be proud of, but the scared little girl inside me still spoke to me in times of duress. In between working a nine to five and a part-time gig on the weekend, I was maintaining a car and apartment, paying real-life bills, and building expertise in my field.

Dating was a whole other story. You know how they say opposites attract? Well, that would be a gross understatement when it came to my male selections. From bad boys to playboys; the jobless to homeless; and, even those with addictions.

I was going through the motions of life, but inside, the little girl inside of me was worried. The little girl inside of me wanted to save the sick and afflicted. The little girl inside of me was overcome with fear and sadness.

I was trying to repress her worries, but the ghosts
of my 'childhood past' kept rising to the surface in
a blur of faces and emotions. It wasn't until a trip
back home for a tragic death in the family that it
all became clear.

The house was full of family members and the soft
whisper of empathetic voices, all trying to console
one another. My mother's throaty sobs had now faded
into the background. It was a sound I thought I would
never hear again, after my grandmother (her mother)
passed away.

I headed to my childhood room in the back of the
house. It was exactly how I had left it years ago
when I left for college. The four-poster canopy bed
greeting me at the door always made me feel like a
princess. The matching white oak bookshelf-dressers
were lined with books, porcelain dolls and trinkets
from every phase of my life, all the way up to the
day I left. As I rifled through the drawers I came
across a small lined notebook. It was covered with
doodles, but in the center of the front cover, was
the word 'Journal'. The memories suddenly came
flooding back. This was not just a book of poetry or
short stories; these were the words of the little
girl inside of me. This was what she wanted me to
confront, to remember, to overcome.

I closed the door, sat down in the rocking chair by
the window, and began to read.

Journal Entry One

Childhood

From a small town down South...

Hi. My name is Tara. Tara Walker. I'm just a child (nine years old to be exact), though sometimes I don't feel like one. I'm one of those kids that was tall for my age. But that's not all. I see and hear things I am not supposed to. Grown-ups are always tryin' to hide stuff from me, like I don't know already.

Trying to be a good little girl is not hard for me. I don't say much so it makes it easy to be the perfect little girl I am supposed to and expected to be. Good in school, no trouble at home, and I eat just about anything, so you can't even say I'm a picky eater. Sometimes I wonder why everyone always calls me "heavy-handed". I guess it's because I break things by accident, and also I'm kind of klutzy, I guess you could say. I'm much taller than most of my friends which makes me somewhat stronger than most my age. This is not something I do on purpose, but I think my mom and dad think that I do. Speaking of mom and dad, I guess you want to know about them, huh? Well, my mom works for this bank in Philadelphia called "1st Pennsy" I think. Anyway, she works all the time and mostly the late shift, so I'm stuck with my brother watching me until my dad comes home. My mom is nice. She's very pretty, and very classy, from what I hear. I try to be like her and also listen to everything she tells me because she's smart.

Sometimes my mom is upset because of my dad. You see, my dad drinks acka-hall (that's a bad drink), and my mom doesn't like it too much. Sometimes their fighting wakes me up and I can't get back to sleep for a long time. My dad's really cool! He's funny and he takes me everywhere. He works at this lumber company where they sell wood and when he has to take me with him to work I get to pretend I'm building all these neat things with hammers and nails. I get lost in my own little world and even forget to have lunch! My dad takes me everywhere! Oh, wait, I said that already. Sorry. Well, this may seem weird to you but I even go with him to the bar. It's a place where all these people meet every day or weekend, I think. They drink that stuff my mom doesn't like and play pool (some boring game with sticks and balls), and video games. Whenever I go there I would drink soda from these tiny little glasses and eat snacks from a bowl and play video games. My favorite game was Space Invaders. Pinball was cool too. Everyone treats me great. It's like I'm a movie star! Whenever I run out of quarters I just get more from my dad. That is my typical Friday or Saturday night. I guess my mom is at work. I don't really know.

Most nights during the week I have to stay with my brother, Pookie, if my dad didn't come straight from work, and most times he didn't. I think he had to get a drink that we don't have at home before coming home. My dad's a good cook and I like it when he cooks dinner for us. I like to help in the kitchen. Unfortunately, my brother (whose real name is Isaiah Jr.) is not a cook. Don't get me wrong, he makes the best french toast in the world, but that's it! I get tired of it every night. So recently I started to just have a bowl of cereal. My brother and I love cereal. We could have cereal for all three of our meals in a day. Oh, I forgot to tell you my mom and dad's names, Rosalie and Isaiah Sr.

Sometimes I wish I had a different family. I love everybody, but things get rather strange sometimes around here. Isaiah is the only brother I have that stays here, but I think he'll be gone soon. I don't know why, but it's just a feeling. My parents argue a lot about him. I think my brother is in trouble or something. Anyway he has tons of friends, because they are always calling and coming over. Sometimes when he babysits me I go over to one of his friends' houses and he goes out. It's okay though, because other kids are there. Most of the time though I just go across the street to the reverends house. He's a round, jolly man who gives me candy and juice and we watch game shows together. The Price is Right is his favorite.

Sometimes I get lucky and one of the older daughters come home and I get to play dress up in their room and listen to them talk about grown-up woman stuff. As soon as my dad gets home from work I rush across the street to greet him with lots of hugs. One funny thing is when my dad drinks that funny stuff, I get tons more hugs. He's funny. But mommy doesn't think it's that funny.

People fight a lot 'round here. I have another brother, Darrell, who acts weird a lot. I think I heard mommy say he was a little "off". I'm not quite sure what that means but he screams a lot. Him and his wife move around a lot with my niece and I heard they fight a lot! Sometimes he comes over here using bad language and upsetting my mom and dad. It is really scary! I mostly just hide in my room in my favorite little corner until it's over. One time he and my brother, Isaiah, got into this big fight and they were punching each other. It started at the front door one Sunday morning. It ended up all the way in the back bedroom, where they busted through the mirrored closet doors. I think my dad broke it up. Darrell left the house mad. After the fight was broken up, my parents called me for breakfast where everyone ate like nothing ever happened.... For some reason, my daddy's home fries and scrambled eggs with cheese didn't look as tasty as they usually did and there was this lump in my throat. All of the sudden I busted out crying and ran from the table to the security of my room. I will never forget that moment. I kinda felt like everyone thought I was crazy and upset for no reason, like I just imagined the whole fight. Maybe I did. Oh well.

My life is filled with school and friends to play with, but I am still lonely most of the time. I taught myself to play games that require two or more people by myself. I can play Easy Money by myself, I can play I Declare War by myself, and I can even play Uno by myself! Playing with my dolls is the most fun. They can talk, they can walk, and they go on trips and everything. I do their hair and makeup and always clean up after I'm done. I think I am very neat and clean, just like my mommy. Speaking of trips, I go everywhere my parents go. My mom and dad take me to fun places with my aunts and cousins some of the time. I go to Virginia to Bush Gardens, and Hershey Park and Kings Dominion and I also go to islands in the middle of water. Most of the trips are planned through this lady at our church. It is soooo hot on those islands! I think I even remember one time when my dad had that bad drink when we were away and mommy got really mad at something silly he did, because it makes him act silly, and they had a fight. But, I was used to it, so it's really no big deal.

Hey, I forgot to tell you about my other brother, Enrique. I call him Ricky. He is truly the coolest. I hardly ever see him because I heard he works a lot and is very busy, but he's fun. Whenever he comes home to see me he says, "Heyyyyyy, how's my girl?", and I get a big hug. Sometimes he brings a girl with him. She's usually pretty cool, and pretty. Vikki was his latest girlfriend. She was really nice and for a while they stayed with me and mommy and daddy, but not for long. When they finally got their own place, I used to visit a lot when my mom and dad had to work. It was kinda weird when I went over there, because they would usually leave me alone or be in the bedroom and never come out. So I would just watch TV or look at some of the magazines they had. But I don't think I was supposed to be looking at them, because naked people were in them and some of the pictures and words were bad. Actually, most of them were bad. I felt bad afterwards for looking at it. I asked God to forgive me and he said he did, and I believe him. Anyway, that was the last time I went over there, because I think they moved after that.

Every Saturday was the same thing. All my aunts and cousins packed up from Jersey and went to my grandmom's in Philadelphia. We had fried chicken and rolls and for dessert we went to the corner store called Frank's for ice cream. I have to tell you about my aunts. They are so funny. All of us just laugh all day. My Aunt Maryanne is truly funny. She tells a story like no one I know. She is the foster mother to all my cousins, Corin, Liza, and Ivana. She is Shana's (another cousin) grandmom. Her real kids are Terri, she does hair and bakes really good stuff; Keenan, he is in and out of jail a lot and makes her cry; and Marvin, the father of my cousins, Mark and Danielle, he has a tire business or something like that and is really friendly. Aunt Maryanne cooks great! She is always taking care of these kids for this agency and then loving them so much she decides to keep them, which is cool 'cause I get more cousins. My other aunt is named Aunt Terri. She is the mother of my boy cousin, Lorenzo. She is always smiling and has this funny laugh that makes all of us laugh even more. She lives in Deptford with her husband, I think, whose name is Teddy. Uncle Teddy drank the same funny drink my dad did and wasn't home much. I think he was a fireman. Don't think I would want him in charge of rescuing me though. Anyway, she seemed happy all the time. I love my whole family a lot.

Anyway, back to the story. This Saturday was no different. After we got our hair pressed at Miss Lucille's at the corner salon we all felt pretty. All my cousins are my favorite playmates, especially Corin. She was my best friend. We all went back to grandmom's that day and ate and went for ice cream afterwards. Our favorite dessert was the wafer ice cream sandwich with the vanilla, chocolate and strawberry all in one. Mmm-mmm good. Ice cream is my favorite. My dad gives me some every night before bed in a bowl. It was always Breyers. I love my dad.

Anyway, after dessert we were all playing and went across the street to Michael's house and played some more. Michael has a crush on me and it kinda makes me blush when he talks to me. Sometimes though he says things about my body I don't like, him and my cousin Lorenzo. Lorenzo is my favorite boy cousin. He is the son of my Aunt Terri. We play a lot outside pretending we're camping through the woods and stuff at his house in Deptford. I kinda look up to him because he's bigger and tells me exciting things sometimes. He has the neatest electronic games. There's just one thing that bothers me. I am not sure if it's wrong or not, but it happened last Saturday. Me and Lorenzo were upstairs at my grandmom's in Philly 'til our parents came to pick us up and he said he wanted to try something and to lay down on the bed. I don't know why I agreed so easily, maybe because I trusted my big cousin. Then he asked me to pull down my pants, so I pulled them down a little to my knees. He then pulled his down and tried to put his thing on my middle part. All of the sudden grandmom yelled for us!! We jumped up, pulled up our pants and ran downstairs. We haven't talked about it since then. I feel really weird about it and I will never tell a soul. That means nobody.

Anyway, let's talk about something else. You know I feel like an only child because I am the only little girl in the house. I have imaginary friends and talk to them all the time. I write a lot too. Stories about all kinds of things, even poems, and let my mom read them. My mom 'praises' me all the time. That means she tells me how good I am. My mom and dad say that I can do anything I want and be anything I want when I grow up and I believe them. I like to sing too. I listen to a song over and over until I have it memorized and then sing it over and over. I like to sing to the songs my brother, Isaiah plays. I forgot to tell you he plays the piano very good, or is it well. Anyway he plays George Benson, "There I Go", Angela Bofield, "People Make the World Go Round", and Patti Labelle, "Somewhere Over the Rainbow". My favorite song was "Black Butterfly". Last Saturday my mom called all my aunts and cousins over to hear me sing it. Afterwards I had to go to bed. I also sang "Street Life". I don't know who sings it but she sings really good. My brother is the best piano player in the whole world and everyone loves him, mostly me. I think my mom and dad do too. Tonight was a bad night for him though. He kinda took my bike and mommy was mad.

Here's how it went - Daddy wasn't here, as usual at night, and she let him have it when he got home. It almost seemed like I was watching it tonight but I wasn't really seeing it. I felt helpless. Mommy screamed she was sick of daddy coming home drunk and then he screamed something else back. The screaming went on for what seemed to be hours. The screaming was like fingernails on a blackboard, cutting into you so deep you kinda shivered. Then I think my mommy broke down. They went from the living room to the kitchen where my mom grabbed a sharp knife and tried to kill my daddy!! Luckily he was strong enough to fight her off, get the knife out her hand and finally calm her down. I couldn't do anything but just stand there staring blankly like this was happening to someone else but me. Afterwards, daddy left and mommy said that I was going to live with her, and daddy and her were not going to be together. I asked tons of questions but I don't think she heard me. She stood in front of her bathroom mirror and rolled her hair in silence. I am lying here in bed now trying to imagine what it will be like to live with just my mom and I am also trying to get the image of mommy with the knife out of my head. I can't seem to sleep. I think I'll get up and watch TV or something. Nah, maybe I'll just lie here.

It's the next morning and no one is acting different. It's like last night never happened. My mom said we are not moving and that was it. That's good, because it would probably be weird just living with her anyway. I wish I knew what the fight was about though. My friend Michelle is coming over today. She's my best friend and she is leaving soon. Her mom and dad are taking her away to Nevada, wherever that is. Anyway, this will be one of the last times we play Barbie together. She loves my townhouse and van that I have. The townhouse has an elevator with 3 levels. I want a house just like this when I grow up. The kitchen is on the first floor, the bathroom on the second and the bedroom on the third. The van had a kitchen, bathroom and bed also. Michelle was tall like me, so was her mom. They were both pretty. She was quiet like me too and was the only girl in the house. She was an only child. I liked playing at her house. I wish she didn't have to move away.

Michelle's dad was a big man with big shoulders, arms and hands. He wore glasses and had an afro like my dad. He was okay. He argued with her mom a lot and I only liked him a little bit. I think he scared me that one weekend I stayed overnight with Michelle. In the morning Michelle and I took a shower together in the big grown-up bathroom with the pretty glass doors. Her dad kept trying to come in the bathroom to see us. I don't like grown-ups to see me undressed. He finally left us alone. Anyway, Michelle goes to school with me too and I'll miss her a lot. Now who will I play dolls with? My mom got her a present for going away. It's a neat alarm clock and I got one too. The numbers are real bright and it plays music. I'm going to keep mine forever! I hope Michelle keeps hers forever too.

In the neighborhood there's not many kids I play with. Mostly the boy across the street, name Ronald and his friend, Varnell. Also, the tall, skinny black girl down the street named Alexia. She was okay some of the time, but one day we were on my swings and she was mean and hurt me and we didn't play together after that. I heard she has a lot of boyfriends already. The other two sisters I played with on the corner were white. I did used to play with them a lot until their dog bit me on the forehead one day. I'm afraid of dogs. Ronald, or Ronnie, is a good playmate. We ride bikes and play in the dirt and swing on my swings together. We talk about everything and listen to music also. He is fun to play with, even for a boy. Somebody told me yesterday that he liked me, but I don't believe them. Boys are yucky and they always look at my body funny. Anyway I don't like boys!

You know, about what I said earlier, about the sisters on the corner that were white. I didn't mean nothin' bad by that. It's just that I hear things and see things. My parents say white people treat us different and that's a fact that will never change, but they tell me not to treat anybody different because of their color. I'm allowed to play with anyone I want. I just wanted to tell you that, in case you thought I was "begadiss". I think that's what my mom and dad call it.

Journal Entry Two

Almost a Teenager

I'm 12 years old now and I'm even more grown up than my age. I write poems a lot to try and express how I feel sometimes. It makes me feel better. My life is okay I guess. Still kinda lonely and sad at times. There is still a lot of fighting going on around here. My brother, Darrell is still fighting with his wife, Jackie, all the time and I think the cops were even at their house last weekend. Oh, and they now live in a house around the corner from us.

I'm learning a lot about my brothers now. Things I didn't understand when I was younger. Darrell is on drugs. That's what makes him act weird. I don't know if Jackie is or not. I don't think she likes me too much. She's kinda mean sometimes. One time I had to rescue my niece from their house because the fighting was sooooo bad! I brought her to my house. Her name is Samantha and she is six years younger than me. Boy does she get me into trouble!! Two weeks ago she told my mom, who by the way thinks she is an angel and loves her more than me, that I kicked her. I told my mom we were laughing and playing footsies and I didn't know what she was talking about, but my mom believed her. I couldn't believe what was happening. I think my mom had a bad day. She scooped me up and threw me on the floor and started trying to beat me with a belt. I ran to my room where she cornered me against the window and slammed me onto the wall below it. I curled on the floor and begged her to stopped beating me. By this time she was beating me with more than her belt and grabbing at my hair. She finally stopped when my niece begged her to. Samantha later told me she could not bear to hear my screams any longer.

I had bruises on my arms for a whole week after that. Anyway, I kinda have to watch Samantha whenever no one is around. I love braiding her hair for her. She looks up to me in a way because I'm her older aunt. I like that. Sometimes when we're bored we make up dances to our favorite songs. We take turns being Debbie Allen from Fame and making up the dance steps. When we're done, we show my dad when he comes home from work. He's been coming home a lot lately without going out, but Friday and Saturday he definitely goes out for his drink. I don't go with him anymore. Actually, neither of my parents are around very much. I just learn to entertain myself. Tonight I have to go over my Aunt Maryanne's house until my mom and dad picked me up. She is the one with all of the foster kids that she takes care of, but to me they're all my cousins. Doesn't matter to me where they came from.

I heard stories from Corin and her sister Liza that would scare you to death. How their mother would leave them alone for days without food while she went out for drugs. They were never bathed or fed. It's really horrible. Anyway, my aunt cooks really good and I was finishing dinner when my parents came to get me. I said my goodbyes and walked to the car. I suddenly got this strange feeling that something was about to happen. I was right. We got home and there was a note on the door. As we walked in, I got the feeling someone had been inside the house. My mother found another note on the table in the dining room. I asked what was going on, because they both were clearly upset, but she wouldn't say. She told me to put my coat back on and that we have to go pick my brother Isaiah up. We ended up at the police station.

I sat in the car and waited until they brought my brother out. He said,"Hi", but that was it. The car is silent, no one is saying a word, and Chaka Khan is singing, "I'm Every Woman", softly in the background. I want to ask what is going on but I can't. That lump in my throat reappears and a tear runs down my cheek.

The next day I hear a conversation I am not supposed to be hearing and what I hear answers all of my questions. My brother was involved in drugs! He actually stashed bags of weed in the floor vents of my mother's house! That's why the police searched our house. If you were wondering, that was what the notes were about. They went through our belongings while we were out, and we had no idea what was going on. As if that wasn't bad enough, this week in school everyone took the opportunity to kindly point out for me my brothers' picture, as well as the article about him, in the newspaper. I really had no idea they printed an article until they told me. Boy was I shocked and embarrassed. I'm glad that episode passed. By next week no one will even remember it. I hope.

You know, my brother isn't all bad. He still is doing this music thing and plays all over town. He is even in a band called "Fat Gary's Band" and they have a song on the radio. It's really neat. I'm just sorry that he messes with that bad stuff. I think it gets him into way too much trouble. Oh yeah, I also found out that my other brother, Ricky, does the same thing. Yes, all three of my brothers put this stuff into their bodies. For what I have no idea. He does the stuff with the needle and goes to bad places in the city to get it. Atlantic City is a really bad place for my brothers to go. My mom says it is nothing but drugs down there, but I don't see any when we go to the beach and the boardwalk in the summer with my cousins. It seems like a fun place with bike riding on the boardwalk, food, candy, arcade games and rides. Not to mention the ocean! Anyway, my mom is always right, so Atlantic City must be bad.

I don't have a boyfriend yet, but everyone says I am too young for that. I don't like them anyway. I still play with Ronnie across the street. Although he did say he liked me one time before, but he hasn't said anything else about liking me. Thank God! Yuck! Anyway, school is fun and I have plenty of neat friends there. I go to Christian School right by my house and I don't have to take that long bus ride anymore like I did when I went to that private school with Michelle, my best friend. The bad thing is that I don't hear from her anymore. The calls and letters stopped and I don't know where she is. I hope she's okay.

In Christian school, we have regular classes and we have Bible classes. Chapel is in the morning. Everyday I have to wear a skirt or a dress to my knees with no slits and pants are not allowed at all. The teachers are nice and all my classes are small. When I first signed up for this school the principal took my parents into his office and after taking their check, he saved us. I felt a lot better now that I knew I was going to heaven after I die. Who wouldn't be happy? Classes were okay and everyday I had a ton of homework. It was hard carrying all those heavy books everyday too.

I'm still tall for my age, but I think I am more normal now. I am slim, I think. My mom watches what I eat, because she says she does not want me to be fat. Candy was a "once in a blue moon" thing and the only snacks I had was fruit, pretzels and wheat thins. Sugar cereals were rare. I ride my bike a lot so I guess I was in shape. Not being fat was very important to my mom, so it was very important to me too. I just want to be normal, even though some of my friends were chubby and they seemed normal. Anyway, they weren't me and did not have my mom watching their every move.

Sometimes Christian school is scary. Did you know that the devil tempts you to do bad things and if you do and don't ask for forgiveness from the Lord you go to hell? Hell sounds really hot and scary. I am a good little girl so I don't have to go there.

I'm in this group called Awana and we gets pins on our uniform for finishing our scriptures and workbooks and projects and get to move to the next level. It's fun and I'm really good at memorizing. Always get A's and B's as my grades in school. Pretty good, huh? I am really good at my catechisms too. My mom and dad always tell me how proud they are of me and to keep it up. They come to all my plays and all my events at school. I have a great mom and dad. Guess you figured that out by now, huh?

Journal Entry Three

Now I'm a Teenager

I just turned fourteen and my grandmom is dead. My mom's mom. I don't really know my dad's mom that well. I guess the trips to Philly on Saturday are done. Actually, they had been done for a few months now. My Aunt Maryanne was taking care of her at her house. Anyway, I woke up this morning to sounds of horrible weeping. Deep, muffled sounds that echoed through the house.... it was my mother crying. It was unfortunate that this was the day before we were to leave for Aruba; my mom, dad and me. Guess we won't be going. My parents sat in the dining room for hours trying to figure this one out. Can they get their money back or not?

I was sitting in my room wondering what the answer was going to be, when, oh wait, here comes my mom!.......oh good, she just told me that me and my dad will go, while she stays to make the arrangements and attend the funeral. I'm gonna miss grandmom. She was the best cook in the whole world and I never once saw her upset or stressed out. I think she was almost ninety years old. But you know, for some strange reason I can't make myself cry. I tried really hard but no tears would come. I wonder why. I was thinking maybe because I know she is happy in heaven with Jesus I guess.

Anyway, my dad and I set off for our trip to Aruba. Just the two of us and my friend LaToya and her parents will be there also. Her parents treat me like their 2nd daughter. They are really cool and lots of fun. Planes scare me a little but I was okay this trip. Well, you'll never guess what happens at the end of this flight. Hijackers!!!! People who steal planes and often use weapons have hijacked a plane on the runway where we have to land!! We circle the air for hours and finally have to go to another airport in Caracaus to land.

Hours have passed, and I am in the airport now exhausted and starving. It is two a.m. and nothing is open. No food anywhere in sight. We have been here for hours with no end in sight. We don't even have our luggage! It was taken to the other airport. Now they just made an announcement that the situation is more serious than they thought and they will be shipping us to a hotel for the night. No food, no change of clothing, nothing to drink. This has got to be a bad dream. My mom saw the report on the news and thought we were on the hijacked plane. She was sooo happy to hear from us. We just called her to let her know that we were all right. I miss her so much right now. I feel kind of lost without her. I sort of borrowed LaToya's mom for the trip; she didn't seem to mind...much.

Sorry to say, four horrible days later with the same clothes on and more broke (so my dad said), we are finally leaving this dump. The S.W.A.T. team went in and got those bad guys. We just arrived at the hotel in Aruba via plane then bus, and guess what?...the rooms are not even ready!! Can you believe this? I just want to go to my room for a minute to freshen up and change my clothes and I can't yet. We ate while waiting for them to finish the rooms.

Finally the trip starts, mid-week. We swim, play tennis, play arcade games, swim some more, play in the blue-green water, run on the white sands, go on tours and eat, eat, eat! What a blast! There was just one small problem. While LaToya and I were having a blast with her parents, my dad was having a blast with some short, light-skinned busty woman who kept trying to be my mother. My dad is a little upset with me because I loudly pointed out to her that she is not, because my mother is not fat and told her where to go. Oh well, he started it! That was the end of her. I'll never be able to get the picture of him and her on the beach out of my head. She had on a bathing suit and he had on a bikini suit. They frolicked around like two teenagers in love. He didn't care who saw him. Not to mention, he never came back to the room all last night. Gee, I wonder what they were doing all night on the beach. Anyway, I am telling my mom when I get home. She has a right to know!

We just landed in Philadelphia and my mom is waited inside the airport. As soon as I see her I am going to give her the biggest hug in the world. You never know the future. It could have been us on the hijacked plane.

We just got home and I can't wait to tell it all. I tell mom the entire story of the 'other woman'. Can you believe that after the fight of a lifetime between my mom and dad, my mom apologizes to me for my dad putting me through the whole thing with the other woman? See, I told you she had class.

Okay, so I'm fourteen and I don't have a boyfriend yet. I do have a crush on this guy though. He is much older and a friend of the boy across the street, Ronnie. The boys' name is Reggie. He is sooo cute.

I don't know much about stuff with boys or girls though. My mom just told me that you should wait until you're married to have intercourse and then showed me some pictures from the encyclopedia. I had no clue what I was looking at. Anyway, I was scared to death of the feelings I kept having and wasn't sure how to even kiss. I think the feelings are hormones, because I kept feeling sore in my chest too. I think I'm getting breasts. And also hair is comin' out of me everywhere. My mom gave me this electric shaver to trim it down. I don't think it's normal to have this much hair.

I hate to jump ahead, but it's now a week later (I get kinda lazy with my journal sometimes) and I found out Reggie likes me too. I rode my bike to his house and his mom just glared at me. Asked me how old I was and all that. She said I was too young to be messing with her son. I think she's right. He is really physical towards me. Not that I don't have those funny, tingly feelings too. We go bike riding to the park and go back deep in the bike trail. We just kiss for hours at a time. Then he wanted more. The kissing led to his hands all over me. Chest, stomach, and lower.... One day it went too far and his hands were inside my middle and I got this exploding kind of feeling inside. It didn't hurt. No, it actually felt kind of good. But don't tell anybody. He can't help it. He loves me so much he can't help but want to touch me. I just stood there and let him do whatever he wanted to. I think he is new at this just like me.

Well, the big day came yesterday. I am fourteen and a half and no longer a virgin, I think. I went over Reggie's house and no one was home. His little brother was in the living room engrossed in cartoons. We were in his bedroom on the bed, about to do something very grown-up like, when he said, "Are you sure you want to do this?...Let me know if it hurts". The next thing I knew he was putting on this piece of plastic on his thing and trying to put it where his finger had been for the past few months this summer. I cannot describe to you the pain I felt. Excruciating pain throughout my middle and stomach! He then took it out and apologized. It was over as quick as it began.

I got dressed, said goodbye, and rode my bike home as fast as I could. For some reason I was bleeding! I washed up and dialed a good friend of mine from school. She is very grown-up with boys and could answer any question. I just know it. She's home, and answers the phone, thank God! She tells me he broke my hymen and I ask her what punctuation has to do with anything. NO! HYMEN! I don't care what it is, as long as I am okay. She tells me I'm fine and to just go about my business. Reggie calls and I decide the whole experience was too much for me and vow to never do it again. Who in their right mind would put themselves through such pain! They must be desperate. I think I'll do what my mom said and wait 'til I am married.

Changing the subject, nothing has changed with the fighting. My brother, Darrell still fights all the time with his wife and is still on drugs. My brother,

Enrique, is still on drugs. And my brother, Isaiah is out of the house, and also on drugs. Am I missing something here? I feel like the outcast because I am not on drugs. This has got to be the reason why my parents keep stressing how proud they are of me and how they can't wait for me to go to college. There goes my freedom of choice. My whole life is already planned. Not that I am complaining but gosh!

My mom still worked at the bank. She and my dad are going into business with this other couple this week. They were going to sell the house and move to a townhouse, just me and them, but I talked them out of it last week. Thank god. This house is my life, where I grew up. No matter how tragic the memories, it's still my home. Now I have to go through this change with this business. I hope it works out. It's supposed to be selling hardware and stuff. Frankly, I don't know why he's giving up that great lumber company job. Oh well!

I have lots of friends and go different places now, but not as many places as my other friends. My curfew is earlier and car dates are out so I am pretty much confined to the mall, movie theater, or skating rink. Otherwise, I am at a church function or over a girlfriend's house, when her parents are home. It's not so bad. I still have fun. The Christian school I'm at is getting kind of lame, but I'm hanging in there. I am just trying to convince my parents to let me go to public school next year. Yeah right. Racism sticks out like a sore thumb here and frankly is getting on my last nerve (I got that from my mom). I really just started to notice it. First, it was the demerit I got for singing a song from the radio - One of my favorite rap songs. Second, it was the scolding me and my other black friends got for talking about the apartheid situation in South Africa that we heard on the news. My parents agree with me but who's to say what there decision will be. My cousins go to the public school I want to go to so they could keep an eye on me, right.

But what is there to keep an eye on? I'm the perfect kid - If there is such a thing.

Journal Entry Four

The Celebration

Time to say good-bye to the Christian school. We had our 9th grade graduation at Mrs. Cleo's house. She was this popular teacher with a huge house on acres of land with a cool pool in the back. Why was she popular? Number one, she was cool, she could relate to the students and was down to earth. You know the type. Number two, she was a natural red-headed bombshell. With her silk blouses and pencil skirts and high heels every day, what was not to admire or like?! I wanted to be just like her when I grew up. Smart, attractive, stylish, sexy...you name it. I could see why the boys and men fell all over her. They could barely speak around her. We would have free time and everyone was supposed to be working on their English assignment. She would be at her desk grading papers. The pencil skirt was so tight I could never understand how she sat down in it and crossed her legs.

She always kept her pencil behind her ear as she graded papers. When she would need to mark up sentences she would slowly remove the pencil from behind her ear, lick it with the tip of her tongue, and write her corrections. Then slowly slide the pencil back behind her ear. The boys in the class were not working after that! Drool was slathered on most of their desks. Gross!

Anyway, Miss Cleo threw us a pool party and invited the other teachers as well. Of course all of the female teachers hated her. They were all quite homely and overweight so you can guess why. And of course the male teachers worshiped her. Her husband was a hunk as well and took it all in stride. Oh and her daughters were gorgeous redheads as well. Bitches. Ha!

So we all having a great time, playing board games inside, pool games outside, and eating everything placed in front of us! Everyone knows I cannot swim so I just play in the shallow end where I can stand. Even though me and my mom took basic lessons at the Y. Still a great time! Even my good friend, Dee, was there. She was the one I called after I had sex the first time; the one who told me about the Hymen thing.

So anyway I was standing by the side of the pool when one of the white guys screamed something inaudible, rushed up behind me and pushed me in the deep end of the pool. Everything stopped. Time froze. Everything around me froze. The more my arms and legs flailed, the deeper I sank. I had no time to hold my breath beforehand so I was losing oxygen fast. At one point I must have gotten back to the top for a second so I screamed "Help!" and took a breath. No one heard my cries. Everyone was laughing and having fun. Why was everyone laughing? I could hear someone yelling, "Very funny Tara, stop playing around!"

I was losing hope but kept fighting my way to the top again. Water was beginning to fill my lungs. Finally, I reached the top and yelled "Help!" again. No time for a breath this time.

And then an angel appeared in front of me and a hand slipped around my waist. I was slowly floating to the top. I can feel air on top of head, my arms, and my legs. But why am I not moving? I can only hear the sounds of chaos around me. A collage of screams, apologies and movement. "What's going on?!" "I thought she was playing around!" "Is she dead?!" "I'm sorry; I didn't know she couldn't swim!"

Someone was carrying me, then laying me down, pulling at my head. I could feel the cool grass under my back and legs. Then there was pressing on my chest and mouth. And that's when it happened. I guess I realized it was not my time. That God had a bigger purpose for me on this earth. My eyes opened wide, I rolled to my side, and proceeded to cough up water. I thought it would never stop coming up, but it did. I was alive and well, but once again the spoiler of the party and center of attention.

Two blessings. My angel, who happened to be Dee. She knew I was not faking since she knew I could not swim. And my old Elementary teacher, who just happens to also be a certified Nurse. The one who saved my life.

So the party was over. Thank goodness I just happened to drown at the tail end of the party. Ha!

This was just one of many near tragedies in my life.

Journal Entry Five

Moving Up

I got my wish!! I got through my first week of 10th grade at public school and life is grand. If only you could see what I see and hear what I hear. They smoke in the bathroom, use foul language, there is no Bible class, no chapel in the morning and boys and girls are pressed closely against the lockers kissing! And their clothes! So tight and revealing! I am shocked, but mystified in the same sense. How do you like my vocabulary? I have gotten much better. I am thinking of signing up for the school literary magazine. Poetry is my favorite. I think I told you that already. Anyway, it still is.

I know it's been a while since I've written, but this journal is growing too tiresome to keep. So much is happening in my life. I am now editor of the literary magazine, loved by my teachers and an Honor Roll student for the third time in a row. The only thing is that I am not very liked by the girls here. They are in my grade, but they just don't like me. They don't invite me to anything and they don't pick me to be on their team in phys-ed. (that's gym). I can only tell you what I have heard and that is that I am a tall, pretty, light-skinned, hazel-eyed, stuck-up bitch who thinks I am "all that". I don't think that's a good thing. Oh well, I just sit in class and wait till the bell rings, hoping the teacher doesn't call on me too much. If he/she does I almost always answer right and that just makes it even worse for me.

Brrrrrrrrrringgggg! The bell rings and I run to my locker, get my books and rush to meet my Sonny. Oh yeah, I forgot to tell you, I have a boyfriend now. His name is Sonny and that is exactly what every day is to me since I met him. I met him through a friend at the Christian school named, Jan. She is truly my buddy. We have sleepovers all the time. Eating Oreos, Entenmanns fudge cake and ice cream all night! What a sugar rush! Chocolate all night! Her mom was cool too. Anyway, Sonny is the light of my life. We kiss all the time and we write poetry and love letters to each other constantly. Today at lunch he gave me a big, soft, squishy teddy bear that he bought from the school store. Last week he gave me a statue of a unicorn (my absolute favorite) that he did in art class. It is gorgeous. He is so creative, cute, and funny. His whole family loves me and everything is wonderful. I ride my bike miles just to see him when I can. As long as I am home before dark. There is just one problem with my boyfriend. He is always in trouble. He spent more time in the principal's office than in class. One time I tried to stick up for him and ended up in the principal's office too. All the teachers were shocked and blamed it on that troublemaker, Sonny, for getting poor little, innocent Tara in trouble.

Well, they were right. Sonny was in big trouble this time. They expelled him Tuesday. I'll never see him now. I still love him with all my heart. I read his letters and poetry over and over. I listen to the songs he sang to me over and over too. No one will ever make me feel that happy and laugh that hard ever again. He still calls and tries to come over, but my parents make it difficult. They say he is nothing but trouble. I think, soon, he will just stop trying to see me altogether. The other half of my heart is gone forever. Not to mention the best kisser alive! He never tried the things Reggie tried. Thank goodness, I still remember that pain.

Oh well, I guess they'll be other guys as passionate as that when I grow up.

I just heard that Sonny was in jail. Something to do with a string of robberies going on in his neighborhood. He couldn't have possibly been involved. That is ridiculous.

But there is another reason for my sadness now. The reverend from across the street died today. Such a jolly old man who loved his home and game shows. The whole neighborhood is sad. I'm not going to the funeral. Those things scare me. Or maybe it's the dead bodies that scare me. I'll miss him very much. I hope they have TV in heaven or he'll be really bored. I don't know much about heaven but the church I go to talks about how nice it is. I go to church in Philly with my mom and dad almost every Sunday. My cousins and I went to Sunday school when we were little, but now we sit with the grownups in the pews. I like to clap and sing the songs. At the Christian church where I went to school, the songs were much slower and you couldn't clap. I don't know why though. My parents cry a lot in church and I think it's because of my brothers and the bad things they do. I have learned to live with my feelings about what they do. I just hold it inside just like my parents; never to speak of the drugs, the stealing, or the lying. I just close my eyes and fade to black.

Journal Entry Six

Graduation

I can't believe this day has come. I am scared to death. Going off to college and being on my own. No mommy or daddy to shield me from the dangers of life. I am hoping to meet some real friends when I go away. I've heard mixed things from people about the dorm. Oh wait, the principal is calling my name. Time for me to hold my head up high and walk up on stage to receive my diploma. Sure is hot out here. The sun is beating down on these bleachers, in the middle of the football field like we are the only focus of its attention. When I finally take this robe and hat off I'll be a new woman! A grown up! A woman going off to college to get another piece of paper. I wanted to go to college. I know my parents wanted me to go for them also. That's okay with me. Whatever makes them happy. I just hope all of these pieces of paper pay off. Some of my graduating class failed, so they'll be in school for the summer and and some will still be there next year. Some are just going to get jobs. And some are going where I am going. Some Cornell, some Rider, some Rutgers, and some Fairleigh Dickinson. There are some who are spreading out all over NJ, NY and down south also. I hope everyone makes it. I get this strange feeling there's a mighty long road ahead of me...

Journal Entry
Seven

The College Years

I'm really gonna miss this house. Visiting on weekends is just not the same as living here. My whole life I had the comfort of this house and the people in it to come home to. Now what? A dorm room just isn't the same thing. The old, brown rancher designed exclusively by my mom and dad made me feel safe my whole life. So what am I gonna do? Go to college as planned I guess....I just packed up, loaded my dad's van, and jumped in. Now, two hours later, we're here.

My parent's unloaded the van, made tons of trips up the elevator, helped me unpack, complained about the room, took me to eat and then left. I'm not one for long, sad goodbyes, so I tried to get it over with. Of course mom tried to start with the mushy stuff. I just told her I'm a big girl now, and can handle myself. If this was the case, then why am I standing in front of the payphone staring at it, dying to call my mommy and daddy. This is the hardest thing I have ever had to go through. No meals, no family, no homework. All of a sudden it turned into "the caf." (short for cafeteria), roommates, and "papers". Papers that in no way resembled the book reports I used to do in school. Help!!!!!!!!!!!!!!

I can't describe the food in the caf. yet. The pasta, bread and ice cream are the only things edible. One thing they shun is eating in the caf. alone. If you were not with a clique, you are strange. Why? I don't know. I heard the meat is processed and all the food is made by mixing powder with a measured amount of water. Yuck! I'm sure you can imagine, we ordered from Dominoes quite a bit.

One good thing is I made friends. At least I thought I did. The black girls were vicious, the black men were horny, and the white people were nerds. My school was only 6% black so you would think they would stick together. NOT!

Anyway, back to college. Very weird things happen here. Sex goes on all the time, people get drunk all the time, and lots of people have mental problems. <u>This place is a psychiatrists dream</u>! There are anorexics, bolemics, suicidals, alcoholics, drug abusers, and rape victims. One Saturday night, in the wee hours of the morning, my neighbor was so drunk and high that she stripped off her clothes and ran down the hallways of the dorm screaming, "Wake Up! Wake Uppppp!" Tell me that a doctor would not have their hands full. Anyway, I am mostly the goody-tooshoes study-holic and never leave my room, or if my room is too noisy, the library. The dorm is really never quiet, so I mostly go to the library. Whether it is music, sex, music, laughing, music, oh and did I say music? Thank God I am outta here Friday.

I thought it would be better in this new dorm with a new roommate. This girl is even worse. She preaches to me about the Lord and scriptures and how she refrains from sex. Then, that same night I can hear her moans and screams of love from her boyfriends' dorm room. Yeah, that makes sense. There were a couple of hypocrites like that on campus. Then she constantly complains about my boyfriend. He is some guy I met off campus at a restaurant. I'm leaving this place in 2 weeks. Getting a rented room off campus.....

Back to my boyfriend, his name is Richard. I asked him why he talked to me the first time he saw me at the restaurant with a group of friends and you know what he said? "I thought you had a cute butt". Can you believe I gave a busboy some play with that response? I must have been desperate, or lonely. The physical rendezvous I was having with the boy on the first floor of my last dorm was fading fast, (oh, did I mention I started having sex again). Okay, so the sex was great, but his girlfriend was still in the picture. (No, I did not know this when we first started rendezvousing.) But after I found out it was too good to stop. Now it was my voice heard down the hall. The brick walls and halls of ecstasy. I was tired of the scenario and plus the girl had no idea she was being cheated on. She was actually really nice (I know because she was in my Science class). At some point, I felt bad and had to cut it off.

Anyway, Richard became my security blanket. He was gorgeous, had a muscular build, and a large penis. Yes, I said it. The sex was even better with him than the rendezvous on the first floor and I was hooked. He never even had to say he loved me. He called me constantly and never let me out of his sight. I found myself practically living in the basement of his mothers' house. This is not something I am proud of because the place is a mess. Mice, dirt and bugs.... Did I mention he had a large penis?? Now that you are caught up I guess you should know I am with him now, while I write in my journal. Which is getting rather thick, if I must say so myself. I'm quite proud of it. Anyway, he is over on his keyboard creating tracks again. He wants to be a musician/rapper (and a busboy by day). What am I doing here? I don't know. My studies aren't being neglected because I do it here, in between love sessions. I've never gone on for hours and hours with anyone. I guess you finally figured out that the pain is gone during intercourse. That went away real fast. Richard helped. I am actually beginning to think that he is the one. The one for what I don't know. He is really nothing but sweet and kind to me but questions are beginning to pop up. For instance, yesterday I made the bed and I found a pair of panties that weren't mine. His answer: "Baby, you know I wouldn't cheat on you. That must have been from a long time ago." My answer: "Yeah, they do look old, like they've been there a while. I'm sorry." You decide, am I dumb or dumber?

Fast Forward a few months. Richard and I are over. He was definitely cheating on me. On top of that he gave me a few things via his penis that I didn't ask for if you catch my drift. That was the last straw. If he doesn't stop calling me I'll be forced to castrate him as punishment. MEN!!!

It's my senior year now and I have been feeling rather lonely. I'm still studying harder than ever and making the grades, but the relationship thing with Richard is getting to me. Neither, he nor myself can't seem to let go. The last straw was the phone call from his new live-in girlfriend. She wanted me to leave him alone. She got my number from the caller ID. He actually called me and left her number for me to call him back and I did. Surprise!! Can you believe the audacity of some people? I can't. Anyway,

I just called my play-brother, Drew, to come over and comfort me and he is on his way. Actually, he is not coming over to comfort me. The truth is I have been suicidal for most of this year. Feelings of wanting to be removed from this earth have been overwhelming me. He is coming to save my life. I don't know where I got the knife that is now in my hand, but it is real, it is in my hand, and it is sharp. God help us all.

I hear Drew's car pull up in the driveway. He's frantically running up the steps and slowly opening my door. At this time I am renting a room off campus on the third floor of a mansion. It was once the servants' quarters. The room is dark and cool. I am curled in the corner on the floor unsure of where I am or what I am doing with this knife. Drew is beside me, shaking me. I can't seem to see him or let go of the knife. I am crying and somehow his face and voice begin to come into focus. I drop the knife and start shaking profusely. He gets me dressed and takes me to the dorm with him to take care of me. That was the last I remember.

I woke up in his bed in the dorm. His roommates never disturbed me. We never spoke of the incident. I didn't want to. Richard was gone forever. No more relationships for me...ever.

Journal Entry Eight

Another Piece of Paper

It is the day before graduation and the whole week sucked. It started off with Richard's new live-in calling me wanting to be my friend. "So what we compared notes and busted his game, you're still with him and I know you're still fuckin' him." Can you believe she had the audacity to call me and invite me to the park?! Just me and her little boy!! I don't think so sista! Anyway, on top of that I am just getting over this horrible cold, and if you think things couldn't get any worse I got kicked out my room.

You see, I had moved to this room in these rich white peoples' mansion watching their kids in exchange for free room and board. It was three wonderful girls and I loved the job and the girls, but to stay there after graduation is preposterous, which is what they required me to do in order to keep the job. It is not like the landlord didn't <u>know</u> I was leaving after graduation.

The year is 1992 and the recession is in full bloom, so no jobs are even trying to drift my way. Not even Career Services at my college could find me a job. Plus this area is all white and they ain't tryin' to hire any blacks. Sorry for the slang. (My mother would faint if she heard what I just said. She loathes improper grammar and English!) As you can see this week has been hell. I am now packing boxes up waiting for my dad to come from down south to pick me up. Can you believe she just told me to leave the day before my graduation?? Shows how much they cared for me.

Anyway, I figure my dad can just take my stuff home, where I'll be moving after graduation and I'll just stay at a hotel tonight. That should be fun. Since I have to be at the stadium early, it was the best decision. My family will be there tomorrow. All smiles and tears I'm sure. Brother, aunt, mom, dad, niece. All there to see the first Walker graduate from college. No pressure here.

I'm in my hotel room unpacking when I get a call. It's the guy from the first floor in my old dorm. You know, the rendezvous. He was making his round of "bootie calls", found out where I was and wanted to get together for a "romp reunion". Hey, I'll probably never see him again anyway, so what the hell. Needless to say he jumped me as soon as I opened the door and it was over before you could say "room service". He was never like that before but unfortunately that last experience left a bad impression. As a matter of fact, after he left I did order room service. And the meal was much more satisfying than the meal my "first floor" romp just gave me. I'm just glad he is gone. I coulda had a V8!

I just woke up. Tired and unsatisfied. No time to masturbate, I'm late already. Hope I didn't embarrass you, but everybody does it. At least I hope so, or else I'm gonna feel really stupid. Anyway, my dress is okay and my hair is just about perfect. I am ready to face the excited crowd, get my second piece of paper and go home with my family.

This is really exciting. I'm standing with some people I hang around with and we're making small talk. We are in lines backstage, so to speak, in the stadium and in groups according to our major. We're all standing around making small talk and saying our goodbyes. Oh shit, now the line is moving and we're going out! I wonder if my hair looks okay? This damn hat is a pain in the ass; wish my mom was here to fix it right for me. She always makes everything all right. What if I trip or something in these stupid heels?? Oh God, my heart is pounding! "Shhh, it's okay", I tell myself. Here I go. Oh my God....Look at all the people in the stands. How will I ever find my family? This place is mobbed. How long do I have to walk before getting to my seat? I know, I'm impatient.

Thank God, we're here. I can sit down. Ooh, my family is over to the left and waving. "Hiiiii!!! Tara!!! We love you.......proud of you!!!" I just know I'm blushing.

This ceremony is boring. You sit down, you stand up, you sit down, you stand up!! What is this church? Anyway, it's almost over. One more speaker and we can go. Yes!!

It's over. My family brings me roses and takes a million pictures. I just want to go back home and out of this town for now. Maybe I'll come back to visit my friends in the nearby towns one day or maybe I will never see them again. Who knows?

I am finally home unpacking and now we have to plan for the big graduation party. All my family and friends will be there. My god sister, Sonya, is supposedly coming. She is one of those people you can't count on. You're just thrilled to see her when she comes and enjoy it while it lasts. She lives in DC now. She used to live in Philly. She took me everywhere on the weekends. I used to sit in bed with her at her apartment and watch TV and eat ice cream from the container. She would sit beside me on the phone talking to her many men. She was very popular. Probably because she was so pretty and had a great sense of humor and a desire to live life to the fullest. Sometimes I feel that way too.

She came!!! My god sister is here and life is grand. I am having a blast. Everyone is here and giving me money! Can you believe it? Whoever invented this rule about money for graduation gifts is a genius! One hundred, two hundred, three hundred....

It's a week later and I am sorry to say, I hooked up with an old friend. He just happened to call me during my party to say, "Hi". He heard I was home from college. His cousin got on the phone to say hello also. I can't believe I used to talk to his cousin. Malcolm and I go way back. He used to date my best friend but she dumped him. He is kind of corny, but I always liked his sense of humor. I was the only one who laughed at his jokes. Malcolm and my best friend asked me to double-date with them, so I got his cousin, Dre (who I swear, back-in-the-day, looked just like El Debarge, the singer). Anyway, he was cute enough and we had a good time, but no sparks. I had more fun plucking Malcolm in the back of the head while he was driving and joking around with him. My friend didn't seem to mind. She didn't like him anyway.

So anyway he calls me up on the day of my party to say hello and off we go. From there we went to the movies, went swimming in his pool, rented movies at his house, and worked out in his homemade gym in the recreation room. It was all platonic until that one day.......

Journal Entry Nine

◆

The Malcolm Affair

You ever get into something that you know is not going to work but you want to try it anyway? This is actually how I felt about me and Malcolm. Light skinned, just like me; funny, just like me; curious, just like me; and passionate, just like me. The only thing was he was short. I have never dated a short guy before. Myself being 5'8 1/2" and all. Anyway our long-lived friendship soon turned into more. One night while watching a rental (movie that is), he tells me he has feelings of strong attraction for me and asked if he could kiss me. I didn't know what to do. He is a good friend, and things have been going smooth for months. Should I take it a step further? Plus, he's short. What am I going to do?

Unfortunately, my hormones and emotions took over and I kissed him. It was the most sensual and passionate kiss I ever felt in my life. I was quivering afterwards and he was 'moved', to say the least. (Shame guys have no way of hiding that.) Then he started reciting this poem for me and that was it. His dad was in his bedroom sleep so who cares, right. (I know....YES HE LIVES WITH HIS DAD AND JUST SO YOU KNOW HAS NO CAR OR JOB AT THE PRESENT TIME, BUT I KNOW THAT WILL CHANGE IN THE NEAR FUTURE OKAY....)

Well, that kiss led to one of the many encounters that would occur in that house. One kiss led to another kiss which led to certain pieces of clothing coming undone. The next thing I knew I was straddling Malcolm on his dad's couch trying to keep my screams and moans from escaping my throat. From the faces he was making I guess he was having fun too. I hadn't been with anyone since graduation so the need for this was there. I needed to do this. So I gyrated my hips around and around until I reached that point of ecstasy that every woman strives to achieve during sex. It just so happened he reached his point at the same time. After the explosions, we collapsed in exhaustion from our lovemaking and went back to watching TV. And that was it. That was how our relationship started.

I admit my love for Malcolm was not as strong as his love for me, but that grows in time, right? Anyway, this feeling of being wanted is great. We write letters to one another, he writes poetry for me, we work out together, go swimming and make love the rest of the time. I can't think of one place that we haven't made love at yet - the car, the plush carpet in his house, the kitchen chair, the garage, the pool and his bedroom. We even made love in the chair at his fathers' table of religion. This is the table where all of his dad's books, bible and notes were. He was always working at that table, but that night Malcolm and I were 'working' at that table.

I even got him one day while he was eating lunch. His dad was right outside cutting the grass and working on his garden. I just maneuvered myself under the table and proceeded to "wet his willy" while he tried, but failed, to eat his lunch. Nothing for me thank you, I'm quite full. Ha!

Anyway, this month things have been getting a little out of hand it seems. He hasn't found a job yet and I have been taking him everywhere in town having him fill out applications. He still has no money and I get nothing for my birthday, Christmas or Valentines Day. But I understand. I always do, don't I?

So now he is starting to drink a little more than I care to say. At parties we're invited to he makes a fool of both himself and me. He, along with his cousin Dre, just get into fights. Either way I get the short end of the stick. He is really nasty and violent when he drinks and his language has much to be desired.

I just moved into my own apartment. Whew! The curfews and checking in every hour was getting on my nerves. I love my parents, but damn! I'm on my own for four years, doing whatever the hell I please and I have to come home to this. Uh-uh! This is not happening. So I move to my first apartment with the money I saved and Malcolm is there helping me unpack. He didn't want to live with me. Says he's not ready. Oh well. One good piece of good news is that he finally got a job and is going to finish mechanics school soon. Thank god he can pay for something now. Although he did make sure to take me out to dinner at a nice restaurant each time he got some money. He went on these truck trips making deliveries and pickups with a friend of his who paid him cash. Unfortunately, this guy was a drug addict and alcoholic and this was really not the kind of influence Malcolm needed. You see, Malcolm was quite wild in his high school years. Dealing with cocaine along with weed and alcohol. He had been clean for a while and had just got released from prison prior to my coming home from college, after serving a 6-

month sentence for assaulting a police officer. Don't ask.

Anyway, I've had enough unpacking for one night and decide to christen the apartment, if you know what I mean. Boy, am I exhausted. It's time to hit the sack.

It's a couple of months later and I'm sorry I haven't written in a while. If anyone ever reads this thing....I don't know what will happen......Things aren't so hot right now. Malcolm is still drinking heavily and I continue to beg him to stop. It seems it is not that bad when he just drinks beer or wine, but gets brutal when he switches to hard liquor, his favorite being gin and tonic. I don't know what to do. He screams at me, curses at me, calls me names, embarrasses me in front of his friends and then minutes later wants to fuck me, telling me how beautiful I am. One morning, after one of his long nights with his cousin he decides he is too hung-over to go to work. The night before, he had promised me that if he went out with his cousin, he would be back early because he knew he had to be at work in the morning. <u>It was only his 1st week on this new job!</u>

Well, he didn't get in 'til 5 a.m. and was going to call out and actually wanted me to call for him! I told him to go to hell and fought my hardest to get him to go to work. It took a long time for him to find this job (with the help of my car and my patience, driving him around to every retail chain and gas station in the area) I didn't want him to ruin it.

54

Anyway, this scenario turned ugly fast. Before I knew it this argument turned into a face-to-face brawl. He was calling me every name in the book and telling me to Fuck off, and I don't remember what I was saying. Then the threats came. I threatened him by telling him I would call 911. Bad move. He was infuriated by this and picked the phone and proceeded to lift it in the air to hit me in the face with it when he stopped. He told me I was lucky that time, but I wouldn't be next time.

Malcolm then got dressed and proceeded to leave the apartment with me following quickly behind. I still had to drive him wherever he was going, work or home. Halfway down the steps he realized he could not find his wallet and keys. He was convinced I had them. When I told him I didn't, he called me a liar and shoved me up the steps and into the wall outside my door. I can still feel the sting on my back as it shook the wall. I opened the door and he went inside and finally found his things after a few minutes of searching. I took him to work.

The next day he called me and asked me to meet him for lunch. He was at work. I met him at a nearby pizzeria and he apologized for his behavior. Said it would never happen again.....yeah sure.

There has been one good thing about Malcolm that I really didn't want to write about. I'm sorry I kept it from you but it is rather painful. This was a very painful time in my life. A month ago my mother had a heart attack. She woke up unable to catch her breath with pain in her chest, or more like a pressure according to her description. Malcolm stayed with me in the hospital the whole time. He let me cry on his shoulder and held me up when I could hardly stand. He constantly assured me that everything would be alright and it was. My mother was only seconds away from death. They said my dad shouldn't have tried to drive her to the ER, but instead should have called an ambulance. She needed the oxygen immediately. Do you believe my mom refused to let my dad call an ambulance because she was afraid of what the neighbors might say?? How absurd! She almost died! When I went into the ER at the hospital I saw that look. That look of death. And it scared the hell out of me. In her soft, yet firm, voice she whispered to me to watch my dad and take care of him while she was away.

You see, my dad depends on my mom for everything. I doubt he can even do his own laundry if necessary. It's okay. I promised her I would take care of him. In the days to come I eventually had to force him to eat. He wouldn't even eat!!

The doctors eventually did surgery, (an angioplasty) on my mom, opening her clogged arteries. She recovered beautifully. I was so happy to have her home. I hung welcome home signs and balloons everywhere. Fourteen days without her was horrible. I couldn't even begin to imagine a lifetime. My dad and I were lost without her. She is truly my best friend. As I got older, my mother and I grew closer. I tell her everything. Nothing is "too personal."

The doctor said he warned my mom a few months ago that her cholesterol was way too high and changed her diet. My dad and I knew nothing about this doctor visit or new diet. But now we know and we intend to make her follow it. No salt, fried foods, excessive sauces and cheeses, etc... We'll do it because we want her around for a long, long time. Because we love her......So as you can see Malcolm supported me at a time I truly needed it and I am grateful to him for that. It was that one kind gesture that I will never forget.

Journal Entry Ten

On and Off With Malcolm

I hate to tell you this, but I am still with Malcolm. It's been almost three years. I think I mostly stay now because I am comfortable. I'm used to him and don't want to get used to someone else. The single life is a drag and I don't feel like looking again for that special someone, if such a person exists! The drinking hasn't stopped. His smoking continues, despite his chronic asthma. And the verbal abuse is still there, sorry to say. He hasn't raised his hand at me since that first time, thank god. But he still scares me sometimes. When he isn't telling me he loves me, his hands all over me, wanting to have sex, he is cursing me and telling me to leave him alone. It's like being with Dr. Jeckle and Mr. Hyde.

I know, you're probably making some kind of comparison to my father. Did that already. The similarities are scary. But I am so used to this life and can't seem to break away. The only thing worth holding on to is the incredible sex. He 'makes love' to me and I can feel how much he loves me. It's quite different from just 'sex'. We have broken up and gotten back together 3 times already. He is insanely jealous and I can't take this anymore. I call him at home and he just sits on the phone saying nothing. I try to talk about the problems in our relationship, but he just nods. I'm nagging again according to him. Well, I am all nagged out. "I gotta get away" like Bobby Brown!

Sometimes Malcolm hangs out with the guys from his job. This one guy caught my attention. Tall, dark, handsome, educated, and worked 2 jobs. Sounds good to me. But I never make the first move. It just so happens Malcolm so kindly got me a part-time job at his store recently. I worked different shifts than him, mostly nights. This friend, named Wayne, was definitely as interested as I was. He tried to tell me every chance he got and I told him I had a boyfriend, and that he knew him. He could not believe me when I told him who it was. Malcolm is not the tall, dark, handsome type. More like short, yellow and lazy.

Anyway, Wayne persisted and I quickly fell under his charms. He told me he was determined to take me away from Malcolm. I was unhappy anyway, why should I care. But I still loved Malcolm. Should I give up a chance at happiness just because my heart is full of love for Malcolm, someone who has made no effort to correct the problems in our relationship? NOT!!!

So Wayne asks if he can come over. He has a car!---"Sure! Come on over!!" We sat on my couch and talked from 9:30pm to three in the morning. We talked about our lives, our relationships, our dreams and our goals. I have never done that before with a man. It was so uplifting. Before he left the apartment he asked if he could kiss me and I said okay. I swear I thought I saw fireworks. The next day I trotted over to Malcolms' house and gave him back his stuff and broke it off. I never cried so hard afterward in my life. It was the hardest thing I ever had to do.

Wayne was thrilled. He came over that night after work and we talked all night again. He said he was falling in love with me and actually called his mom from my house to tell her. He put me on the phone with her and everything. Can you believe it? After he left I felt like the whole night was a dream. I was all smiles and giddiness the next morning. Like a teenager. The same way I felt with Sonny. He had even spoken of marriage last night.

Malcolm called this morning crying. Begging me to forgive him and take him back. I turned into a person I didn't recognize for a moment. I told him it was over between us and it was not like we were happy anyway. Just give it up. Then I hung up. He never called back or spoke to me at work again. Soon thereafter he quit. Got a fancy job in his field, mechanics, over at the local Bus Company. Now he makes some money! (Boy, my timing is off!)

Well, come to find out it was more than just talk (about marriage). Wayne popped the question. First to me, and then at a formal dinner in a restaurant with both our parents, which he paid for. I was all smiles again. He moved into my apartment and worked day and night. The other job was nights at his mom's job, Anchorage Mental Hospital. He watched over patients...making sure they didn't get away I guess. I had been there with him, to pick up his check. Everyone knew about me and congratulated us. I guess you figured out I said yes.

So here's the thing though. We hardly see each other. When he comes home he sleeps. We both agreed to wait until our wedding night to have sex and so far so good. But the questions keep popping up - Questions about his whereabouts after work, his schooling and much more. Of course, I ignore it all like most women trying to be trusting and supportive...until that day...

Everything fell apart that day, week, whatever. It's all pretty much a blur to me. I thought things were kind of strange but chose to ignore almost all of it. But one day I couldn't ignore it any longer. I searched his things and found nothing incriminating except a bank account that had less than twenty dollars in it. His bank account was supposed to have thousands of dollars in it, along with some valuable CD's. Obviously, this is not the case. I decided to check the college he went to for proof of his law degree. They sent a list of graduates to me from that year. No Wayne on that list. Another lie. Then I called his job. He hadn't been there all night. Another lie.

Ready for more? He told me about some land he bought where our house would be built. I pulled some strings with some realtor friends of mine for some info. The land didn't exist. Shall I go on? Instead of acting hysterical I quietly packed his stuff up out of my closet, threw some in his bags and some in large trash bags and lined it up neatly at the door. He finally called and I told him to come home and get his Shit and get the *!@& out of my house and my life forever.

When he pulled up I was balled up on my bed crying. Trying to figure out why this was happening to me. He didn't come right inside. He sat in his car listening to his favorite song, Kenny G's "The Wedding Song", quite loudly. When he finally came in he said nothing. He left, and I hurt. He did attempt one more lie before he left. Told me that he was not at work because he was at his fathers' house in Delaware and that his father gave him the thousands of dollars he needed to buy the land where our house would be built, and that if I had not thrown him out and been so irrational I would have been able to share in the good news with him. Do you believe this bastard?!! I did. But only for a minute.

A day later I actually begged him to come home and give our relationship another try, but he refused. Said he wasn't ready. I hurt him too much. This son-of-a-bitch was crazy. I tried to verify the information about the money and his dad's generosity with his mom and she laughed. Guess that answered my question. Anyway, I hurt for a while and so did my parents, but we got over it. I sold the ring, paid some bills and vowed to never let a man trick or fool me about anything ever again. You'll see later how well I did with this vow.

I won't tell the rest of the story in complete detail because you might hate me. After being dumped by me and watching me with another man, Malcolm wants back in. He calls me. We talk. He wants to see me. We fuck. From then on it wasn't much of anything. Sex held it together. He said he didn't think he could be with me again because I hurt him too much when I left him for Wayne. What did he think he did to me for three hellish years?? I can't imagine what goes on in men's heads sometimes.

Anyway, it was a sort of arrangement we had I guess, which would ultimately come crashing to a horrible halt.

Enrique, my brother, is not well. I think he knew for a while. Remember I told you about the needles he uses to take drugs? The drug known as heroin? Well, it seems he switched to 'crack' too late in life. The sharing of needles was already the major cause of death in thousands of people from a disease called Aids. Since then, my mother and I have been taking care of him since he got really sick.

The girl he was living with for six years threw him out like a piece of used clothing. She had no use for him any longer. She was a drug user too. "Crack" got her. Introduced to her by an old boyfriend. She never stopped after they broke up. What's worse is her occupation......<u>she's an elementary schoolteacher</u>. You can close your mouth now. You heard me right. Anyway, so far she tested fine. Lucky her. The funny thing is that they met in rehab. Came out of the program and went right back to it. They said it was like the drug was calling their name and they had to answer.....I didn't bother to ask if it was possible to ignore the call and send it to voicemail....

Anyway, my brother is ill. His hair got real fine like baby hair, real straight and curly and soft, and his feet swelled up making it hard to walk. He just basically got weaker and weaker. I would get his food for him or his drink, which was cans of Ensure. Gotta have nutrients to keep you healthy... He's in denial. He knew a long time ago. He could have gotten the AZT drug to prolong his death. Any extra time on earth is good, right?

It's been months now since I've written. I apologize but life has been hard. I can't land a good-paying job. People actually offer me high school positions for minimum wage. I thought my degree meant something. Just started this data entry job for $6.00/hour. Enrique is worse. It won't be long now. I'm trying to be strong for my parents but......it's so hard......I am trying......I just can't accept the fact that he's ....

I'm sorry I couldn't finish. I'm in the hospital with my brother. Nothing to do but read something or write, so I'm writing. Every time he comes here they send him home. Says there is nothing they can do. The disease is too far gone to administer any drugs. I don't believe them!! There has to be something!!! Please tell me there is something!!! I sit here and watch the clear bag above his bed pump morphine into him like water and shudder at the mere thought of being drugged to die.

You know he made death come quicker right? My brother actually continued to smoke 'crack' until the week before he died. Said he could care less, he was going to die anyway. How could he say that? "Hello!!! There are people here who love you and want you to live as long as possible." (Sorry, the tears are running down my cheek and I need to get a tissue. Sometimes they start rolling and never stop.....)

Journal Entry Eleven

The Phone Call

It's almost nine in the morning. I'm up. Just lying here staring at the ceiling. Not really asleep. Clouds are slowly passing over my apartment as if to make a statement. The phone rings. I hate to answer it. It's my mom. Ricky passed away at three this morning, while I was so selfishly sleeping. My mom, dad and my brother, Darrell, went to the hospital to identify the body. I'm glad I went to the hospital the other day and told him I loved him. It would be unspeakable if he died before I got to say that one last time.

Enrique was the brother I was the closest to. I could always talk to him about life, problems, men. On Christmas and my Birthdays, he was the one brother who remembered me. His gifts were special, meaningful, and from the heart. A special person and good man has left this earth.

I said, "No", at first, unable to accept the news. Then I just cried. Just like I had been doing four weeks straight now. Except this time, my cry was more like a painful, moaning wail that swelled in your chest like a balloon and gripped your throat like a vice. My mother tells me to be strong, get dressed and come over to be with the family. I do it.

I walk in and death is in the air. A dark, metallic, bitter smell I can't describe. I can barely breath. I can't even speak. I can taste the salt from the tears rolling past my cheeks and my nose and into my mouth. Darrell hugs me first. Then Isaiah Jr., my dad, then my mom and the rest of my family.

Just to let you know, Darrell had a heart attack right after my mom and it was massive. He continues to eat wrong, smoke and drink regardless, which led him to his second relapse. At least the drugs are out of his system. Guess he didn't have a choice. Anyway, he is really upset and I worry about him. Just like me, he has a temper, and is rather hyper, so I have to really try to help him through this if I can. But who will hold me up?

Anyway, Isaiah Jr. and his girlfriend (play wife, mother of his kids, or whatever) were talking about getting their life together and how this has taught them a valuable lesson. Let me tell you, this girt 'T' that he has been with forever, living around the corner, in the house my mom co-signed on, is sick. She grew up in a dysfunctional family, with drugs, physical and sexual abuse by her mothers' many boyfriends and it screwed her up in the head. She has tantrums, even when she is not high on drugs, and she curses and screams at my nephews and abuses them as well.

Myself, and the teachers at my nephews' schools have witnessed the results from the abuse. Bruises, cuts, you name it. Anyway, I don't say much because I've heard this before and I am still a little ticked at them not coming to the hospital to see my mom when she had her near-fatal heart attack. They'll never give up the 'crack'. The addiction rate is so high it scares me to hear about it. He even does it with one of my other cousins, Lamonte, on my dad's side. He is the same age as Isaiah; the only difference is his wife is a church-going woman, not a druggie with him.

My brother and cousin both have the same characteristics: can't keep money, can't keep a job, habit first ...pay bills second. You know the symptoms. This death won't make him stop either. I hope I don't sound too cynical.

The day before the service everyone comes over to visit. The whole family gathers together for strength. Even the family members that were too scared to visit Ricky when he was alive, because they were afraid they would catch "IT", came to our house. I couldn't bear to look at them. Those ignorant people. Enrique never did anything to you. And you can't catch Aids by being in the same room anyway.

Why do people bring food to the grieving family's home? I know we don't have the time or the energy to cook for everyone. It's a nice gesture; I just wondered how the tradition got started. Anyway, each day the Entenmanns would sit on the table with fried chicken, cakes and pies along with other dishes that would sit on the table for dinner. I am the host for my mom. Serving, cleaning up, helping, etc....

My cousin Lamonte drives a limo as a job now. He drove us to the church. We cremated Enrique and Darrell wants the ashes. I think they want to sprinkle the ashes in the ocean. That would be nice. The memorial service was planned as a tribute to my brother. I hope I can get through this. I can't seem to stop shaking.

I can't tell you the details about the service. I lost it. I tried to hold it together and failed. Everyone was there, including my god sister from DC, my second parents (Latoya's mom and dad), and even all my cousins. I met people I didn't even know. It's really all a blur to me anyway. I lost it as soon as my brother, Isaiah, started playing a piano solo for my late brother. This dedication utilizing his utterly breathtaking talent made me lose control. All that talent wasted on what continues to kill our black men every day in our society----DRUGS!!

I'm sure you can understand why I lost it.

Back at the house.

More food and desserts...More flowers...More people. I change my clothes and continue to play host. I tried to cope for me, my mom and my dad. I'm okay for a moment and then lose it again. Trying to understand "why" is the hardest thing. You keep asking yourself if it was something you did or something you could have done.

Enrique spent his last days in my old room in my mom's house and I haven't been able to sleep in there since then. I just kept going back to my apartment and coming back early in the morning. I guess that may sound kind of silly. Oh well.

Everyone keeps telling us to hold on and be strong, move on and don't mourn forever, but no one is telling us how. Maybe they don't know either. We'll make it through this, I just know it.

I went back to work. A week was all I could afford. I told them my brother died of cancer. People are very ignorant about the disease, AIDS, and I couldn't afford to lose my job because my boss thought I would be a health hazard to the office, simply because I hugged, kissed, and fed my brother on his deathbed. What is this world coming to? Why are our minds so closed? Scared of things we do not understand, I guess.

I don't know how soon I'll be able to get over this sadness inside me. I'm trying my best.

Journal Entry Twelve

Back to Work? Maybe...

Back at work everyone is asking questions. They want to know how my brother got cancer so young. People are so insensitive. I just tell them I can't talk about it and do my work.

This job is so stressful. I started out in the data entry department just to work. The pay was only $6/hour. After working there for a few months, there was nothing left for me to do. I am a fast worker and have always had a problem with stretching one task out for a whole week, when I could easily finish it in a day. The manager calls me in and says he can lay me off or I can take the job in the insurance department as a medical biller. Well, let me tell you about that department before I tell you my decision.

Remember high school and the jealousy, competition, degrading comments towards your peers for a laugh? That is the insurance department. It is located on the other side of the office and directly next to the collection department, where they scream at people about paying their bills. These women, a majority of them black, were crude. They cursed, backstabbed, and criticized on a daily basis. They were either moody or cranky all the time about something in their pathetic little lives and it showed in their behavior, speech and attitude. Now, let me tell you what my decision was...

I just could not stand to go on unemployment so I took the job as a medical biller. I thought my Christian attitude and bright smile would get me through anything. What was I thinking?

People like me got beat up in school by bullies, and stepped on by the bad and the ugly. I was the kid with no backbone; the kid who lost their lunch money every day and got teased because of my pretty clothes and close relationship with my mom and dad. I couldn't survive this. No matter how much I smiled and stayed positive, they tore me down. Literally, I was torn apart limb by limb, until there was nothing left to tear apart. My self-esteem and positive attitude had been shot down. I was conscious of the way I walked, ate, wore my hair, dressed and spoke...

I remember that day as clear as if it was yesterday. I ran out of the office with my pocketbook and coat in hand, hysterically crying....they had initiated the final plan for my destruction.

Lemme set the scene for you. It was a cold, brightly colored conference room with mahogany furniture, cushiony swivel chairs with gold rollers on the legs, and plush rose-colored carpeting. I always liked that room, usually used for board meetings or employee meetings for departments, but this particular day it felt as though the temperature had dropped below the freezing mark.

The whole insurance department was called into an emergency meeting as soon as I returned from lunch. At first I was worried, but then I thought rational. I had just received a high review and raise the week before and also been complimented on my fast, hard and efficient work just that week. So why did I feel sick?

I guess the plan worked well for them because I left a half hour after the meeting began. Made-up conversations and boldface lies shot back and forth across the room like a game of tennis. My neck moving with every volley. I thought I would have whiplash. I tried to interfere, to dispute the lies with truth, but to no avail....I could only shed tears...in the midst of crises one can only shed tears...when face to face with Satan I could only shed tears...

I left that cold, brightly colored conference room that afternoon, but <u>not</u> before saying that God is with me and that all I want to do on a job is <u>my job</u>. I always, and I mean always, do my work, finish my work, and then help others finish <u>their work</u>. What I wear, what I eat, how I dress, or how I wear my hair, should not be an issue. I left the room shedding tears again.

And so my journey on faith alone begins.

Journal Entry Thirteen

The Job Market

Sometimes I think of what those people did to me, but I try not to dwell on it. The Lord always seems to take care of His children. What's that old saying? Oh yeah, "What goes around, comes around." Their time will come when they will have to appear before God and account for their actions.

Ever since I have been out of school the job search has been rough. I just can't seem to find any place worth staying. The pay is terrible and I have to work 2 or 3 jobs just to survive, (mostly telemarketing at night and on the weekend.). And by "Survive" I mean pay my rent and utilities, and eat. So as soon as I got out of school I registered with agencies and applied to a million places in the paper. Still I found nothing.

It seems the prejudice in this world is something definitely holding me back from succeeding. My degree is in Business Management and Marketing, and I can understand not finding a job because of no experience, but entry level jobs paying $7/hour should be giving me a chance at least. I just know I would do a bang-up job, as I always do. Even my family knows this for a fact. When I put my mind to something, I do it. Not half way, but all the way.

One of my older cousins, T, got me a job for the summer one year at her government office and I did <u>so well</u> and finished the job <u>so fast</u> that I received an award at the end of the summer. I was truly honored. Anyway, I decided to check the paper as soon as I left the insurance company. As luck would have it I found some really great customer service jobs paying enough money to keep me on my feet until I found a good permanent job. I was trying to get something using computers, because I had been using them since school and found them fascinating. I learned a lot of new programs since college too.

The year was 1996. I had all this creativity and thought I could start my own business as a freelancer for extra money. I registered the business, doing graphics, such as color business cards, flyers, presentations, etc... I'll tell you about that later. So I called the different places and made appointments. Now keep in mind, most of the jobs were through agencies and most minorities know the deal with them. If they have not experienced it, they heard it on the news. The client lets the agency know by use of a code whether or not it is okay to send a minority in to fill the position, or if he/she wants a white male or female only. So my chances were slim from the start.

My last stop is another agency. Great. I walk in and expect to be stared at and patronized once again.

Journal Entry Fourteen

The Career Path

After working several administrative temp jobs, I finally had an epiphany. Since I finished the work so quickly and was usually bored for the rest of the day, why not use that time to master the software applications on the computer systems?! What a great idea!

So I set out to access every feature, menu, and option within each program, from MS Word to Excel to PowerPoint. I took notes, created and completed practice exercises, and tested myself. I was on a mission!

My next role was in the field of technology. Configuring quotes for the IBM AS 400 machines. I learned quite a bit in this role and actually became the go-to person for all new hires entering the configuration department. Teaching them everything about the AS 400 machine and creating these handy little user guides with instructions and notes for success in their new role. I don't remember how long I was there but at some point, maybe after a year or so, I decided to apply for some of the advanced job roles within the company. I had the degree, experience, and job skills for the job. Surprisingly the job went to a younger, white female with no degree and no experience. Go figure.

You will see that this will be the pattern for almost every corporate job role that I will possess. I overachieve; get the highest ratings on my work performance, attempt to advance, and am shut down. Period. Can prejudice be this prevalent in the workplace in 1997?

Journal Entry Fifteen

Filling in the Blanks

I'm twenty-eight years old now and I've shared my most intimate experiences with you. Or so you thought. You can see that I had a good childhood in terms of a nice home, wonderful parents, nice clothes and the best schools. Yes, there was chaos from my brothers, but it did not really affect me directly. Or so I thought. Notice the trend here?

You are probably wondering if I was happy. I was always a happy child, smiled a lot, very polite and respectful. But was I happy? Yes and No. I was happy in my home in my little world, sitting in my room reading, writing poems and songs, listening to music, or practicing my singing, but socially I was not. Meaning the lack of friends even within my own family, specifically my female cousins, made it hard to 'feel good' about myself. It was always the green eyes of envy that took over all of my female relationships. And I was already a very sensitive person to begin with. I used to get all self-conscious when my mom would tease me calling me "funny-lookin'" or grimace at something I had on or something fattening I was eating.

I'm just plain tired of people criticizing me for my looks, my clothes, and my accomplishments, as if I could stop being light-skinned or start dressing ugly and like a slob to make them happy. Or perhaps I should stop making the Honor Roll for them. Would that make you happy bitches?!! I am who I am and that's all there is to it. I admit that because of how people judge and criticize that it has been a lonely life so far and I'm sure it will continue to be one far into my future…at least when it comes to female associates.

So, here's the thing, I feel bad about a few things I left out and I really wanna to keep it real with you. First off, there was an incident during one of my trips home on the weekend with an old friend after the breakup with Richard. We went to high school together and always liked each other. But the bottom line is that he was a bad person. He sold drugs, conducted robberies, and made runs along with other incidental misdemeanors.

So one weekend some female 'associates', not friends, invited me to a pool party at his uncle's house. I don't think he knew I was coming. I don't swim as you know, but I put on my bathing suit and looked cute on the side of the pool with my feet dangling in the chlorine-filled water. We barbecued and mingled. Of course, I was always the pretty loner, aka weird one. So my 'associates' left without me at the end of the night supposedly going to another guy's house for an after-party, whatever that means, and I had to get home because it was almost midnight and I was staying at my parents. Can't get in too late you know, or they'll freak out.

So he offers me a ride home. His name is Linc by the way. He says he has to stop by his house for a minute so I said okay. Told him I would wait in the car but he insists I come in for a minute. The house was dark and quiet, so I assumed everyone was upstairs sleeping. We came into the house from a side sliding glass door, which placed us in the living room area.

I sat on the floor on my towel, instead of the couch, since I was still wet. Then I sat patiently while he went upstairs to change or pick up whatever it was that he needed. I told him it was after 11pm and I had to get home soon.

When he returned he smiled his most charming smile and sat on the floor beside me. He said that he had missed me, and wanted us to get closer and proceeded to move in for the kill. It's not that I did not want to kiss him but I was hoping that was where he saw this ending as well. I really wanted to wait in the car anyway. We kissed and I said I had to go again. He said just one more minute and in one strong move, even though he was a tall, thin guy, he swooped me down flat on my back and was on top of me. I didn't want to wake up the household so I loudly whispered NO! Get off of me! and other words of rejection. His hands were everywhere trying to get into my bathing suit and soon, as I got louder, his hand was over my mouth.

I had no other choice...I bit him.

He jumped up cursing and told me to come on he was taking me home. Said I wasn't worth it anyway. He drove me home and I never saw him after that. Least he drove me home, right? That night I showered for 45 minutes until the hot water completely ran out. I scrubbed and scrubbed but couldn't get the dirt off of me. I thought I'd never feel clean again.

So that's that. I bet you are probably figuring that there can't be anymore, especially after hearing about the attempted molestation from cousin Lorenzo and the attempted rape by Linc. Well, guess what? You are wrong.

Okay, here it goes. You know how I told you about how I used to ride my bike everywhere when I was younger, especially around my development, called the P section. Remember my Aunt Maryanne's son Marvin? At one time, him and his wife and kids, Mark and Danielle, had a house in our development. We used to ride bikes together to the corner store all the time and there was even a pool. It was a great above-ground pool that I was tall enough to stand in; therefore, I wasn't scared to play in it. I was okay when it was Danielle and me but as soon as Mark jumped in I became a bit uncomfortable. He and his friends were always leering at me. Or should I say my body. I didn't understand it at the time but I understand it quite well now, as an adult. What I didn't know was how far it went. Let me explain.

It was a hot summer day and Marvin was there while we all played in the pool. It was time to get out and Marvin had made us some hot dogs for lunch then said he had to go out for a while. I was just going to change and ride my bike home. I just came out of the bathroom and went looking for Danielle to say good-bye but couldn't find her. The hallway upstairs was full of bedrooms and bathrooms and they were all open, except for one.

My feet were like lead, but I lifted each foot one at a time and walked slowly towards to the only closed bedroom door at the end of the hallway. As I got close there were muffled noises coming from within. I couldn't decipher any words though. I

86

called out for Danielle again and the door swung open. I immediately started backwards and asked what they were doing. Danielle was smiling and said they were playing a game. Mark leered at me in his usual way and asked me if I wanted to play. I asked how it was played and Danielle said it doesn't hurt at all and that I just had to lie still and not make a sound for five minutes. She said she plays the game all the time with Mark. Wanting to be accepted so badly and not look like a scaredy-cat I said okay.

So Danielle goes out into the hallway and Mark shuts the door. He says to lie down on the bed. Now here is where my memory blacks out a bit. I don't know if he fondled my breast with his hand or mouth, like it really makes a difference at this point, but I do remember him pressing his penis on my pubic bone and making a lot of moaning noises. It lasted for a few minutes and then I got up and ran out of the bedroom. I could not get home fast enough! Danielle was standing in the hallway smiling and saying, "See I told you it wasn't that bad." I felt like I was going to throw up right then and there. I grabbed my swim stuff, jumped on my bike and never entered that house again.

I went home, showered and changed, and never spoke of it again. My cousins and I drifted apart after that. I think they were just happy I never told.

That's pretty much it for filling in the blanks. Now competing in my adult mind are thoughts of inadequacy, sexuality, and self-worth. Yet I continue to smile, work hard, get degrees, be independent and make my parents proud. They say I am

all they have to live for since my remaining brothers
are drug addicts. No pressure there. Piece of cake!
Ha!

Journal Entry

Sixteen

The Dating Scene

One day I was just minding my own business when I met this guy in the record store. I know, what a cool place to meet someone, right? So we started talking about music and tracks and he tells me about his producer dreams and his studio. I told him about my voice, singing dreams, and the usual curriculum vitae of my life.

We end up at a diner having the best eggs and hash browns I have ever had in my life, and talking for hours. I think I may have gained 5 pounds that morning. Well, after that, we were in it to win it! I took my songs that I had been writing my whole life, and he helped me get them copyrighted. We made tracks, wrote melodies, sang, practiced and sang from morning to night almost every day I had off from work and all weekend.

He had his own modest home in Camden at the time. He also had one son by a psycho baby mama, and a bucket full of problems with the law. I should have run the other way, but instead chose to get involved with this man who worshipped the ground I walked on. It's nice to get that kind of attention, you know? When I sang, the way he gazed at me with his jaw dropped, was a look I'll never see from any other man in my life. Little stars and hearts sparkled from his eyes. For real! Not little dollar signs like some men.

Anyway, I went for it and very soon we were making tracks, music, melodies, and love. Intensely passionate love that made my toes curl. Although he was short, he was a football player for the township and was very, very, very much in shape and muscular in all the right places, if you know what I mean.

And his stamina was unheard of for men his age. Our longest session was 3 hours. Amazing!

Guess you want to know the name of this musical genius, football player stud. His name was Jaheem. Life was good. We took turns staying over each other homes, made music, worked and made love. I knew all his friends, everyone turned out for the talent shows, and we were almost done with the demo. And then the drama came...from the psycho baby mama.

It was he said, she said, phone call threats and hang-ups from the psycho girl, and accusations of infidelity. Then it got more complicated. Fights broke out, guns were drawn, and I felt my happy little musical world crashing around me. I knew the accusations against Jaheem were true because every time we made love he left me presents. It was nothing serious, but unwanted just the same.

So one day I am sleeping peacefully and when I awoke I had a horrible dream from the night before take over my thoughts. Now let me explain my dreams first before I go on. Ever since I was small I have been a very emotional person. I feel things from others, such as auras and energies, and I dream visions that are symbolic and sometimes match what is going to happen in reality.

So I had this dream that Jaheem was using the bathroom when the police barge into the house and dragged him undressed out of the house in handcuffs. It was horrible. That day, at 6pm the phone rang. It was a collect call from a correctional facility. It was Jaheem. Everything in my vision was true.

I don't want to get into the reason behind the arrest but the point is I was willing to stand by him as long as I could. After only a month of phone calls and letters, Jaheem called asking me to move on with my life. He did not know how long he would be incarcerated and wanted me to be happy. I cried and pleaded but to no avail. His mind was made up. He said that there were dangerous people involved and he did not want to put me in danger.

And so I moved on. My tracks and music, except for my songs, were lost forever.

After only two months the bank foreclosed on his house and he lost all of his possessions.

So back on the dating scene I go. I meet people here and there but it never amounts to much. I've moved to two apartments since we have last spoke. My dad calls me a gypsy 'cause I move so much.

Since everyone was talking about the Internet for dating and meeting people, I decided to get this new service called DOL dial-up and give it a try.

So I start out with this web site called Black Planet and started to review profiles. Everyone seemed so professional and nice. I was also checking out the profiles on DOL Dating as well. A few of the guys emailed me but I quickly learned to weed out the perverts and losers, or so I thought.

There was this one guy who seemed nice, almost sweet, and we began exchanging emails. I decided to share my new Internet information with Louanne, a friend of mine from an old telemarketing sales job. We were pretty close, to say the least, and we always shared new guy info with each other.

Okay, so here's the deal. Louanne is my crazy, cute, white girlfriend that every black girl has. Right? Anyway, we do everything together, movies, restaurants, talk on the phone for hours. I've talked her out of suicide once or twice, and she's consoled me when I was down in the dumps about money, a man, my mother (a whole 'nother story), or whatever.

One day I come by her apartment for dinner with her and her man and after he goes off to the bedroom to sleep off his drunkenness, I run out to my car to show her this new toy I ordered. I know, you are slowly beginning to think I am some kind of freak or nympho or something, but I swear I am a nice girl. :-}

So I open up the box with Louanne and we both sit and stare in amazement. There in front of us was the biggest clear plastic gel-like cock we had ever seen in our lives. It was a dildo so it had a strap with snaps on it. So we both look at each other blankly. I did not know this was what I ordered. I really thought I was ordering a dildo without the vibrator piece to it. So I spoke. Someone had to. Louanne was caressing it like she was in love. Her mouthwatering like it was a Hot Fudge Sundae. (We both loved ice cream and Friendly's, which automatically made us best friends.)

So anyway I spoke. I say, "We should try it out!" And she says, "Really!" And I say, "Sure. I'll put it on and try it out on you." So we get naked and try it out. I think it was the best sex she ever had. She sat on it facing me, and then turned around away from me, and I used it on her from the back. She actually orgasmed! I think I did too actually. That thing makes you feel like you are man with a penis and really in control. Now I see how men feel during sex. Ha! Her boyfriend never woke up the entire time.

So for an hour after we sat talking on the couch about our sexuality, Louanne was convinced that both of us were secret lesbians that had just come out of the closet. Not me. I like men and that thing they like to swing! Yessir! Thinking back on it now, I find it hysterical. It was a one-time thing that never happened again. Things did get a bit weird after that though. Louanne talked about it too much and I think she may have even wanted to do it again. Maybe she was a lesbian. Or I just hit it too good! Ha! Now I really see how men feel when women chase after them after good sex.

Okay, so Louanne and I are scanning the DOL profiles together and she actually found a few nice guys she dated from there. And of course I met my sweet guy in person finally. Louanne insisted on being in the restaurant with us as a safety measure. She was a good friend, always looking out for me.

Dinner got off to a rocky start but eventually turned out okay. My date was very shy and could barely form a sentence without stuttering and grinning for the first 30 minutes. I really thought he was going to knock over more than one drink, but we escaped with just the one spill. How embarrassing. He was definitely not as refined as his profile. It seemed to me like he was not used to being out in public with women at all.

I have to ask a question. How is it that if I am so good at reading people, auras, and energies, that I cannot run the other way when losers come my way? I'll have to check with Steve Harvey on that one! Ha!

Bio on Mr. Not-together, aka Loser, aka Rojer. Just lost apartment, lived with mom, no full-time job or career, no car, and no money. So why did we connect? Things in common include looks, computer games/interests, eating, and, oh yeah, don't forget loneliness. Two Ha's! for this one. I must give him this though – he doesn't drink alcohol or do drugs. And he is kind of sweet in his own kind of way.

So after a few hours we ended our date. I dropped him at the train station so he could go back to his mama's house and that was that. Louanne called that night to make sure I was safe and asking about how it went of course. I told her he was nice, we had good conversation and that was it. No hot chemistry, no talk of him being 'the one', or anything like that.

Rojer and I emailed and talked on the phone after that. We played computer games together and hung out at the movies occasionally. Somewhere down the line I met his mother because I had to pick him up and that's where he lived basically. It was a rather strange relationship on first impression but hey what did I know. The point of this whole thing is companionship. We were both lonely, nothing to do and liked a few of the same things. Eventually we also had sex in common, and that was pretty good, so I guess that would be one more thing in common. To be honest, I was still really hurt about the whole Jaheem breakup from months ago.

So his mother lovvvvvved me and actually when I think back on it, seemed a bit **too** enthusiastic. So that day we were going to his old apartment to gather more of his things. It was a crappy part of the city. You know the type of buildings that smelled of urine and fried chicken? Anyway, have you ever heard of hoarders? There's a show about it on A&E now. So I walk in and basically could not walk in any further. There were boxes, furniture, trash, computer parts, clothes, and more, everywhere. What exactly were we picking up again? He then tells me that he had been ordered to clean it out or he would be fined and the rest disposed of. First of all, I was looking h-o-t that day to hang out later, so moving this whole apartment was NOT in my plan. Secondly, he told me we were only picking up clothes.

Of course somehow he suckered me into taking a few loads of boxes to the dumpster. Once I began to perspire that gig was done. I was lookin' too ka-yute to be gittin' all sweaty and stuff. So I waited in the car for over an hour for him to take as much to the dumpster as he could and for him to get most of his clothes, packed up in my trunk and then we headed back to his mom's house.

His mom looked like she was about to have a cow when he brought all that crap from the car to the house, but what could she say. Her house was pretty packed to the hilt as well. Not "hoarder" material but definitely had the potential to grow into one. The living room area and the whole upstairs were closed off. Yeah, it definitely had hoarder potential. Anyway, after unpacking my car, we headed out to visit some of his relatives that were having a BBQ/Birthday party for one of his cousins.

It turned out to be a nice day and everyone of course lovvvvvved me and told him over and over I was a 'keeper'. Frankly they seemed almost shocked that he brought a female over at all. Weird huh?

We spoke of his son and I met him a few times as well. He was nice and polite and we got along well. He was mostly into computer games as well. Like father like son.

A couple of weird things were invading my thoughts but not enough to break things off. He was not allowed to pick his son up at the door of his aunt's (mother's side) house. There were some female cousins there that were 'scared' of him and had accused him of doing 'untrue' things to them. He claims the girl was mentally disturbed and lying. I had no reason to not believe him so I let it go.

Then one time at the movies we were coming out of the theater and walking to the car when Rojer completely froze up as we walked past this male cross-dresser who was staring at us. I had NO idea if he knew him or what, but again I asked if he was okay, and he said yes, and that he was fine. I certainly never questioned his sexuality before. It never even crossed my mind.

So we dated for a while, he stayed at my apartment and I stayed in his room at his mom's a couple of times. Why not more? It wasn't the cleanest of habitats and again the relationship was a bit weird with his mom. One morning I woke up and Rojer was not beside me. I got dressed and went to look for him and he was in his mom's bedroom that she shared with her live-in boyfriend when he was around. What was weird was that the TV was on and they were talking but she was half naked sitting in the chair next to the bed. I knew she was an alcoholic but it was the a.m. so I knew she wasn't drunk. Can you close up your gown please? Hello, your breasts are out! Weird right? I excused myself and went back to our room.

And one other thing I noticed is that his computer time topped mine by a lot! Mostly playing Spades. Eventually we went out less and less.

One weekend we were staying at my apartment and were in the middle of our "love sessions" when something did not feel right. After he was 'finished' he looked down at the condom and there was a slight hole in it. Yikes!

I panicked! I don't want a baby with this guy. I don't want to rush anything. Maybe I'm not fertile! Oh god, I don't know, I've never been pregnant before. Unlike my friend Dee, who was the female definition of the Fast and the Furious. She had four abortions and 1 miscarriage by age twenty. Double Yikes!

So I rush to the clinic the next day and consult with a physician. He thinks I am definitely pregnant and suggests I take the morning-after pill to eradicate the issue. I rush outside to call Rojer and ask him his thoughts. Would he hate me if I take the pill? He says he respects any decision I make but wouldn't mind having a family with me as well as a new child in his life.

This is definitely not for me so I take the damn pill as instructed.

No sooner than I get back and lie down does my stomach and head start to turn. I run to the bathroom and glance in the mirror and I am green. Literally! Less than an hour later I begin vomiting. This went on all afternoon. I had to get back to the Doctor.

A few days later the Doctor consults with me again. After a urine test he determines I must have threw up all the medication and it did not take. I was pregnant.

Shit! Excuse my language, but Shit! I never wanted a kid this soon, especially without a husband. Now what? This kid must be some fighter, determined to come into this world. I try to remedy the situation and she said "Fuck that, bitch, I'm coming out like Diana Ross!" Ha!

So I called Rojer from the car and he was actually excited. He wanted a family, wanted to marry me and

raise our child together. So I said, "What the hell!"
and decided to give it a go.

Journal Entry
Seventeen

---◆---

From Engagement to Marriage

Rojer was working part-time for the government processing returns, so he diligently worked every hour he could and gave me all of his checks to save for the rings and wedding reception. We were going to have a small wedding ceremony with a minister in my parents' home.

I guess you are wondering what my parents thought of this whole thing? Not good. They had their feelings of doubt and skepticism from the beginning, but I was happy and in love and could care less. Oops. My bad. But hey, that's how I felt.

Eventually we were able to save up for everything and began to make the arrangements and bought the rings. It was a happy time for the most part.

One weekend we went up North to visit his brother and for me to meet his brother's wife and kids as well before the wedding. They were very polite and friendly and made me feel quite at home.

Unfortunately, I learned quite a few things about his brother and their mother on that day as well. While Rojer and his brother had actually been estranged for a while, his brother Bryan and his family had also been estranged from the mother for reasons unknown at the time.

Weirdness #1: The wife was overly submissive to the brother with _Everything_. She would say things like, "Can I get up? May I use the phone? Can you lay out my clothes for dinner?" I was completely in awe. I mean, I certainly wait on my man and serve company food and drinks when they come over, but I can

CERTAINLY dress myself. She even asked for his help with lipstick, but was not <u>allowed</u> to wear any other makeup.

Weirdness #2: Bryan, his brother, sat me down and said that he had something very important to tell me. I thought it was about the scar on his head. He had a brain tumor removed 5 years earlier. But it wasn't. Rojer is nervous and just nods the whole time. Obviously intimidated by his brother. Bryan says that their mother is a mean and vicious person and was an alcoholic their entire childhood. He said they were victims of horrible abuse and were hospitalized many times and it has affected their lives and relationships. He then told me that he wrote her a letter confronting her about it and asking if she would join him in therapy but she refused, denied anything ever happened and tore up the letter. He and Rojer were very hurt and Bryan hasn't spoken to her since.

Well! This is a strange first meeting. So we all go out to dinner to eat, laugh, drink and be merry, and that was the last time it was spoken of.

A month before the wedding Rojer moves into my one-bedroom apartment. We were planning on moving to a bigger two-bedroom apartment before the baby came so he/she could have their own room. I was hoping for a she so I could dress her up in pink frilly dresses and braid her hair. I think Rojer was hoping for a girl as well. Although he had a teenage daughter, he really just found out about her and never had a hand in her child-rearing. That's a whole story in and of itself for another day.

Guess you are wondering how Rojer and I got along in that one-bedroom apartment huh? It was interesting. We worked and saved money, but in the down time I was training my fiancé on Microsoft Office programs and helping him redo his resume. He was the kind of man that required a little bit more guidance than others did. So I cooked, cleaned, did the laundry and kept him focused and organized.

His resume was a work of genius, not to toot my own horn, and we began sending them out to the various companies in the area. Rojer would spend hours submitting to the various job sites. We were shooting for getting him into IT (Information Technology) as a tech support person at a Help Desk.

The wedding ceremony was weeks away and I had to work with my mom to select a reception hall, purchase the dress, and set up the ceremony in my parent's home.

My aunt took care of selecting the minister, a friend of hers and a neighbor. Check!

We found a dress that would cover my pregnant belly and yet not look frumpy or baggy. Check!

And lastly, we found a hall down the street from my parent's house that was luxurious but in our price range. And the food was great! Check!

The last step was the rings. My dad took us to the city and we were able to get a great price on a wedding band set and engagement ring.

Onto the wedding...

Journal Entry Eighteen

The Ceremony

I guess you can tell I was more excited about the baby and pregnancy than the wedding ceremony. It's not that I did not love Rojer, but I just was not 'in love' with him. But the mothering, nurturing, caregiver side of me kicked in and I truly did believe he would make a great dad and we would make a great family. He was so excited about the baby it's all he talked about. He was constantly feeling my belly and kissing me.

So the day comes when our immediate family, parents of both sides and my aunts, and of course the minister, meet at my parent's home. The reception isn't until Saturday.

There are flowers everywhere, and the home is bright with love, even though the sun is shining only halfway today. I smile at Rojer and he smiles back at me. We both agree that we are doing the right thing.

I duck into the guest bathroom for one last pep talk in the mirror. "Okay, Hooray!! The day has come and you can do this! 1-2-3 break!"

As I am exiting the bathroom, my parents catch me in a last ditched effort to change my mind. I guess they realized I was going to go through with it so they let the notion go and then hugged me so tight I can feel my skirt seam starting to stretch and hopefully not pop.

Everyone takes their place. The minister does his thing and we repeat after him every solemn, dictated word, from the scriptures of the Lord above. Everyone began looking around, when it got to that certain spot that everyone knows so well, to see if anyone would speak out when they should really be holding their peace. Rojer and I looked around at all the family and friends in attendance and then back at each other, all the while smiling and praying for no interruptions. After the vows, we were pronounced man and wife and were given permission to kiss. Even though my belly clearly showed we had passed that base long ago.

Time for celebration! We eat and chat for an hour or so and then everyone goes home. Great news was waiting when we arrived.

Journal Entry Nineteen

Better Days Ahead

Rojer checked the voice mail upon our arrival, and while I was changing, I noticed a huge smile spread across his face. It was a Help Desk job he had applied for and they wanted an interview! We were so excited.

Before his interview we practiced his Microsoft skills and role-playing customer service and interviewing skills. He was good at smiling when he wanted something and I was sure he could ace this and get the job. It was through an agency that I had a relationship with. They actually emailed me for the job and I passed it to Rojer.

I just knew that if we both had good jobs and loved each other we could make this work. He was my husband now and I would have done anything for him. What I didn't realize is that his future and desires differed from mine. I'm beginning to realize that many of the people I meet on a day-to-day basis are very different from me and their personality traits are different as well. I'd consider myself a naturally happy person, I love laughing, and smiling, and many people around me are or seem to be so so miserable.

Saturday was the reception. My cousin T helped me with my makeup, the salon did a great job on my hair earlier, and everything was running smoothly. The flowers, photographer, and the limo arrived right on time.

It was supposed to be a time of celebration. One of my distant cousins from down south congratulated me in the lobby, but not before asking if I knew what

I was doing because I haven't known him long enough in their view…Really? First of all she was the last person that should be giving advice. Her men consisted of married men (like her mother), abusive men, alcoholics, and a variety of losers. Basically we were all adults and have to make our own decisions in life. Don't hate, just congratulate. Right!?

So the announcement is made and I can hear the DJ from the lobby announcing us. The happy new married couple that is. We walk through the doors and the crowd is on their feet. Tears of joy and smiles a mile wide greet us with love. It was the best feeling I ever had in my life.

I danced with my dad and everyone else, smiled for a million photos, and thanked everyone for their support (minus my cousin of course). The food was great, the DJ was amazing and in the end it was a joyous occasion for all of us...until it was time to cut the cake.

Although we hid it well, Rojer and I got into a minor tiff about how to hold the freakin' cake knife, the photos that would be taken during the cutting and feeding of the cake, and how to feed each other. I was so embarrassed, but he had no etiquette or shame and was being completely childish insisting on doing it <u>his</u> way. I could feel the eyes on us as it occurred. The whispers that they knew it was a mistake if it started off this rocky.

Anyway I smiled my way through and pretended it never happened. Despite the heartburn from the baby, I slept good that night with my new husband.

Well, I like to see the glass as half full and so I assumed better days were coming. Rojer got the call after the interview and was offered the job. He took it of course and now we had to find out how he was going to get there. Since he had no vehicle he had to rely on public transportation, most likely buses.

Once he figured out the bus route he was so excited. He could not wait to start his new job.

A month or so later we received more good news. We were approved for the apartment in the complex we were admiring and could move in within a month.

Things were progressing, we were spending time together; a few disagreements here and there, but nothing major...yet.

Journal Entry Twenty

Troubled Days Ahead?

Great news! We are all moved into our new apartment. I am so excited to have a 2-bedroom apartment with a washer and dryer and even double sinks in the bathroom. Even though I had to put everything under my name because of Rojer's bad credit, I was still thrilled.

My parents and one of my older cousins helped decorate the nursery and donated the new crib and changing table. It was truly a blessing. Rojer was working every day and giving me most of his check every week. We had extra money to decorate, buy new clothes, and still hang out on the weekends. Things were going better than expected.

Unfortunately, after a few more months passed, it all came to a halt. Rojer's focal point became the TV and the computer. And it doesn't help that the computer desk was in the living room facing the TV… Perfect! So this is supposed to be one of the happiest times of my life right? But, the walls are slowly closing in on me.

It started with the temperament of my husband. When he came home after work, he was too tired to help me with any of the household items, such as carrying a laundry basket or reaching for something on the highest shelf.

In addition, my brother Darrell had continued to live his life in the fast lane and his heart just could not keep up. He was on his second major heart attack and his doctors recommended he be placed on the transplant list. He would become a permanent resident of the heart transplant ward of the hospital until then.

Not to mention, the difficulties I was having with my pregnancy. I was placed on bed rest for the remainder of the pregnancy. Almost 3 months left - to be exact. Between visiting my brother in the hospital and trying to stick to the diet and bed rest plan for my pregnancy, and don't forget those finishing touches that were needed in the nursery before the baby was born, I was s-t-r-e-s-s-e-d! The one nice thing I do remember is the closeness of my family during that time. Everyone coming over to sit and talk with me, help out, pitch in, and just love me, was a great feeling.

With all this going on, (prior to the Dr.'s orders), along came a guy named trouble. He was spontaneous, deceitful and sneaky. He invaded our lives from every angle. It was Rojer's evil twin brother. A side of him no one knew existed, except maybe his mother.

Rojer found it harder and harder to get along with others and began getting into personal disagreements with his peers. Although he was very professional when speaking with customers and excellent at resolving their technical problems.

I was feeling frustrated at 8 months pregnant. I was also feeling alone, which is something a newlywed should <u>not</u> be feeling. Sex was non-existent because I was huge and it was hard to find a comfortable position without tremendous back pain. Rojer and I were in the middle of a heated argument when I threatened to call my parents and tell them how he

114

was treating me, not helping out with the heavy lifting per the Dr.'s orders, and ignoring me at night. He was even having his dinner at the computer desk now. Rojer was obviously s-t-r-e-s-s-e-d as well and temporarily forgot I was 8 months pregnant. He grabbed the phone from me and shoved me against the wall. The pain shot up from my legs to my belly, the wind was knocked out of me, and I fell onto the bed.

Rojer was so scared I was going to <u>really</u> call my Dad or 9-1-1 that he ran from the apartment.

I called my parents and told them what happened. Silence filled the line. They were afraid their initial fears were coming true.

Rojer turned up late that night and slept on the couch. He apologized the next morning, I packed his lunch as usual, and he left for work. The incident was never spoken of again.

Journal Entry Twenty-One

Red Alert

It was a hot summer night, tomorrow was Labor Day, and my parents left the weekend before on their annual cruise. The previous day, Rojer and I had been back and forth to the hospital and this morning it was the same thing… false contractions. The doctor said I had to dilate more in order to be admitted. It was painful and extremely frustrating. So, we continued to drive around and go back and forth as we waited for my body to do what it was supposed to. Aunt Maryanne drove us, all hours of the night and to and from the hospital because Rojer could not drive since he didn't have a license. Again, that's a story for another time.

Tonight, I knew was the night. I could just feel it. The contractions were coming even harder and closer together. I was heading to the bathroom for my 5th potty break in an hour and I told Rojer I thought my water had broke. Surprisingly to me, when I went into the bathroom I found bright red blood and not water all over my clothes and in the toilet. I screamed to Rojer to get the doctor on the phone right away! I was petrified to say the least. This is not what I expected to find. This can't be happening a week before the baby was due.

The doctor ordered us back to the hospital right away. My aunt, once again, rushed us to the emergency room. I was in the car and then a wheelchair screaming like a banshee. You could hear my voice echoing loudly throughout the hospital building, the hallways and the corridors.

Once we were in the room, they broke my water with some type of long yellow hook, which scared me more than the epidural needle that was soon to come. I looked at both objects as if to say, "What the hell do you think you're going to do with that!?"

All I could think about is my parents and how they would be returning from their cruise and would probably miss the birth of their granddaughter. According to the doctors, I would be giving birth on Labor Day with my aunt and husband there to witness. Good thing my aunt Maryanne had a great sense of humor because my husband…his ass was about to get stabbed. Ugh!!!!

Over the next 11 hours of labor I sucked on ice chips, screamed, watched the contraction monitor and screamed more, passed out from morphine, crapped myself, screamed from simply looking at the epidural needle, and then went numb from the waist down.

Then after all that, some crazy doctor comes in to replace my regular doctor at the last minute, I have no idea why, and he is a royal pain in the ass. Not only is he 4-foot-tall and hitting on my aunt, but he is cracking knock-knock and other dumb ass jokes the whole time. I don't have time for this shorty! I have a watermelon trying to come out of me and I can't feel my extremities in order to push the damn thing out! So shut up and do your medical doctor shit before I kick you in the face!

Aaaaaahhhhhh, that feels better. Release the s-t-r-e-s-s. Wish I knew woooo saaaaa at the time, but it had not become popular or known to me until years later.

So, as I said, 11 hours later a glob of white and red glob slid out of me and I slumped over completely exhausted. I didn't see any of it. The mirror they kept telling me to look in was a black shadow to me. At the doctor's request, my husband cut the cord and they "swooped" my new baby girl away. I felt like I had just been run over with a monster truck and I didn't want anyone, especially my husband, to touch me. And yet they kept stroking my head and shoulders and telling me how lucky I was. She was 6 pounds 9 ounces of joy and I only needed two stitches and had a bad case of hemorrhoids. Did I mention I crapped myself during? Ugh!

All cleaned up and labeled with a white band, they bring our daughter over to me. She was beautiful. We named her Destiny. She has soft black curly hair and was so light-complexioned, she was red. And she had the cutest button nose, and alert eyes. She was everything I could have dreamed of… but boy could she scream!! Wow!

No sooner than 30 minutes after we all took turns holding her, did my mom and dad fly into the hospital room! "Mommy! Daddy! I'm so glad you made it. I just gave birth!" My aunt had called their cell after they got off the ship and told them to come directly to the hospital from the airport. And they made it to the hospital even though they had to fly from Florida where the ship docked.

So everyone came to the hospital to see my precious gift from God. Everyone got a chance to hold her. We took pictures and fussed over her and the nurse brought her into my room for feedings as much as possible.

I haven't slept since that day. Ha!

Journal Entry Twenty-Two

What Happened to the T in Team?

Every little girl has this same childhood dream, or something similar, at least I think so. A knight in shining armor sweeps the princess (that's the little girl) off her feet and takes her to live in the castle happily ever after.

Okay, so now here's my dream. I meet and marry the man of my dreams, we live in a cute little 2-story house with a white picket fence and backyard with swing set, take trips together in the summer, and have sex frequently. Okay, so I just added that in. But so what.

So I find myself at a loss when this precious baby who's cute face and curly hair...SCREAMS NON-STOP. The doctor says she has colic. She was allergic to the first 4 formulas, with the 5th being the charm. Lactose intolerant they say. Something told me to breast feed.

I'm tired, cranky, and ready to drink. I have a little help with laundry and cooking and cleaning from my mom, bless her heart. Her and my dad work from home, even though they are supposed to be retired, and so they have the time to contribute.

My husband says he works all day and refuses to get up in the middle of the night for feedings, refuses to ever change diapers and forget about baths. Although he will hold her while he plays on the computer or watching TV. Of course they are usually inappropriate shows like Smack-down wrestling...you know, shows that I don't really want her seeing...ever.

So here I am, all alone, yet supposed to be married and working as a team.

By week 6, I pass out from exhaustion. I couldn't take it anymore so I packed my bags and went to stay with my parents. Me and Destiny were away from home for the first time. I think I slept for 3 days straight. My parents got up with Destiny every time she cried. Wonderful and supportive parents are a blessing from God for sure.

By the end of week six, we were headed back home. The husband demanded it. Says he was going to help out more but that never happened. At least I always knew where to find him….At the computer desk playing Spades - at least I think, and watching TV as well. And don't forget eating. My husband was not of the thin or slim body type. But then again, neither was I.

Size was just another item us women had to go through. I went from a size 10-12 to a size 22 W. Shopping in the plus size stores was the most depressing moment for me. I walked with the stroller at the park, joined the gym, watched my food intake, but nothing worked. Finally, I had the doctor prescribe a water pill for the excess water I had retained and that seemed to actually help. I was slowly draining, so to speak, like a sink with an unplugged, yet tiny, drain.

I remember so vividly that last sonogram. Destiny looked like she was doing laps in an Olympic size swimming pool. I actually saw the fluid; like waves in the ocean. It was incredible. No wonder it was so hard for women to drop the pregnancy weight. Most of it was probably fluid.

Anyway, back to the teamwork bit. I gave 80% and he gave 20%. That's fair, right?

At that point I just accepted it, but not without a bit of resentment. But I still loved him and I would do anything to make it work. He still reminded me of that stray puppy or kitty cat who shows up at your door with this sad face and nowhere to go. I had to give it a home. Otherwise, it would be lost.

Journal Entry Twenty-Three

Skeletons in the Closet

I t was a perfectly cool, yet perfectly warm, spring day. (Sound familiar?) Rojer had gone into work to do some overtime on this Saturday. I decided to clean out some of my junk from the storage closet. Only a few boxes belonged to Rojer, which he brought from his 'mama's house'. There was one box that caught my eye. I was always anxious to look at Rojer's work from his photography side-business. He took great wedding and reception photos. I just didn't like the work he did for women, creating sexy calendars for their boyfriends.

I was casually strumming through the wedding photos when I uncovered a stack of stray photos at the bottom of the box. To my surprise, it wasn't photos of women. Need I say more?

Destiny was in the playpen next to me. Suddenly my vision blurred and the room started spinning. The stack fell out of my hand and splattered on the floor. Naked men with girls in disgusting poses in some dark bedroom; with only the flash of Rojer's camera to illuminate the worst parts. Then the final nail in the coffin…Naked men in provocative poses staring lustily into the camera lens as if they were lusting for Rojer and he was feeding into it.

What was this? What kind of pervert was my husband? My stomach was turning and I was afraid I would turn over my lunch. I threw everything back in the box, shut the closet door, sat on the couch, cried for a bit, as I waited for my husband to get home.

Rojer knew when he came home that something was wrong. I asked him quietly, "Who are you?...Do I really know you?"

He immediately went to the computer thinking it had to do with that, but I hadn't even put that together yet at the time.

I told him what I had found in the box and he downplayed it to death. Said it was from a photo shoot and that he does not do that anymore. (Do _what_ anymore?) He also said he moved those old boxes from his mama's house and had forgotten about them.

I wanted to ask him why he was photographing men and if he was gay but was too scared of the answer and/or the response. I was a coward playing with fire.

We argued. I told him to get that smut out of the house and not to bring it into our home again.

When he went to work Monday I took a trip to my parents' home. They were excited to see Destiny but knew my face displayed fragments of pain. They knew it was something to do with Rojer. They had sensed it before we even married. They always had this bad feeling about him, just never truly wanted to voice it or acknowledge it. I mean how do you tell your little girl that the man she was about to marry, might not be as "straight" as she thought. I could see why they wouldn't say anything.

They weren't surprised by my findings but were as disgusted as I was. We all sat around watching the beautiful Destiny giggle and smile...not a care in the world.

A week later I got a panicky call from Rojer from work. He had accidentally cc'd a distasteful joke email with pornographic content to someone in his group that was a Christian and very opposed to that type of material. The co-worker reported it to the manager and Rojer was written up. This was his final warning so it must not have been the first time something like this had happened.

I'm beginning to see a pattern here. Let's see if you can help me put the pieces together. Although the beginning of the relationship was calm and quiet, a pattern has begun to emerge that exhibits the following:

selfishness

unable to care for self; need for direction

long computer hours

pulling away from intimacy

homosexual photographs

pornographic material

In addition, the patterns continued to progress from the home to the workplace.

I was seeing that cup again, and it was still half-full. I was sure I could save this puppy...and my marriage.

Journal Entry Twenty-Four

Talking

Why is it that every therapist's solution to a faulty marriage is talking? Maybe we just need to fuck more. Ever think of that Mr. therapy man?! Huh!?

Anyway it was not even a year yet into our marriage and we decided to seek counseling. Communication, consideration, compromise. The 3 C's that solve all your problems. It only works if both parties are willing and able, and both parties weren't.

I tried really hard, I really did. With my credit, again, we bought a townhouse, closer to my parents. It was beautiful. With a driveway, garage, backyard...3 bedrooms and 2 ½ bathrooms. I loved it. It was me making a new start with my new husband and new baby. Our new home was a fresh beginning for us.

We were entertaining our families, having barbecues and Christmas parties. Everyone was jealous of how fast we acquired a new home with the baby and all. It was heaven.

And then I woke up.

Oh yes, there were parties, but the smiles that were "plastered on" as the "happy family" were all fake. Afterward we would turn smiles into frowns and go right back to arguing. About everything. From his socks in the middle of the living room, to not helping out around the house when I needed help with chores. If I asked for help on the weekends with vacuuming for example, he would wait until Sunday at 10 pm when everyone is sleep to do so. It was infuriating.

Although, I have learned now that compromise and patience was my weakness back then, and that a jacket left on a chair instead of hung up in a closet, is not going to bring the world to an end. Ha!

So we argued and argued and he spent more and more time at the computer. Believe it or not, he sometimes was on all night and never came to bed. If he did, it was the wee hours of the morning and I was zonked out.

One night he was so into what he was doing that he did not hear me step into the office where the computer desk was. He quickly tried to close the pop-up window he was viewing and typing on with naked women displaying their "goods" plastered on the screen. I had suspected as much.

The arguments exploded into full-blown violence. I was scared for Destiny…scared that the yelling would have a negative effect on her. Doors were slamming and things were being thrown, and worst of all, Rojer was beginning to put his hands on me again.

I was now a bitch, a drug user like my brothers, a whore, and much more. I was no longer a good mother, beautiful, and smart. Or was I?

Rojer was the type of man that could hold a grudge until the next century. And you could see the anger in his face while he held onto that grudge. It would eat him alive.

So the pattern continues. No talking, no compromising, no sex, no success in our marriage. Our therapist's dollars hard at work.

So much for talking.

God bless my parents again. They stepped in and tried to counsel me and Rojer. Trying to hear our side of the story and present us with examples of how they had made it together for over 40 years.

So much for talking.

Our last visit to the therapist was a sad one. I've never in my life heard of a doctor or therapist or counselor saying something like this.

He sat us down and told Rojer and me that he felt this marriage had no hope. That the scars went too deep and that certain parties seem to not want to change their ways. He suggested we part ways and move on.

Journal Entry
Twenty-Five

Me & Destiny

It was now just me and Destiny. A few weeks later Rojer had moved into a 1-bedroom apartment which was down the street …about 20 minutes away. I could tell Destiny could sense his presence gone from the home. She would sometimes sit in her crib and scream dada over and over. Until she realized he wasn't coming to pick her up, or make her laugh.

You see, in essence I believed in my heart that he loved Destiny, and even me, but mostly Destiny. I believed that he would truly do anything for her, would protect her, and keep her safe. He would spend hours videotaping her, as she took her first crawl, and then her first steps, as she played. He would sit with her watching TV and she would sit quietly in his lap for hours. She loved him so much...unconditionally.

So life goes on. While I was at work my mom babysat and after a while she was ready for the day care scene. My parents were getting up in age and she was quite a handful.

Destiny and I went on trips together to the park, the beach, and other places. Her little cousin, Lorenzo's daughter Niecy, yet in the care of Aunt Terri because of his drug use, came over with Aunt Terri often. The two were only a year apart in age. They would play in the backyard in the little (blow up) kiddie pool in the summer, splashing and laughing for hours. I would cook hot dogs on the grill and we would enjoy the afternoon chatting about everything until the kids conked out in front of the TV watching children's videos.

Rojer was granted "every other weekend" visits at his apartment and I actually worried about his ability to care for her since he had never participated in baths and diaper changing in the home. I was a bit taken aback when he picked her up one weekend and greeted her with, "Heyyyy Sexy". Why would a grown man call a 2-year-old sexy? I commented that I felt it was inappropriate, but it fell on deaf ears.

Many times she returned home with diaper rash and other marks. He said he had everything under control so I let it be, for a bit.

I have to admit I would have felt more comfortable if Rojer had a girlfriend. At least there would be a woman, who knew how to care for a baby girl, helping him.

The incidents got worse and after a frightful emergency room trip I had to take charge. She had suffered from scratches and bruises and a broken wrist.

The mother urge in me to protect my child kicked into overdrive and I decided to take my case to the courts.

This time I had no money for a lawyer, having spent all I previously had on divorce lawyer months earlier, and even that I had borrowed mostly from my parents. So in I went headfirst into a sea of motions, or what the courts call 'pro-se'.

Day after day, month after month, I filed the necessary paperwork. There were court appointed exams and reviews, more paperwork, more hearings, and more stress. At one point the judge was kind enough to offer a parenting class to Rojer in case he needed more guidance with bathing, diaper changing and so forth. He declined. Said he was fine.

How could we ever go on with our lives until this was resolved?

Destiny's safety and happiness was the main concern here. She was screaming more and more, hiding in closets, playing in her feces at home and in daycare, and extremely aggressive to the other children. Every week I was leaving work to pick her up from daycare, and sometimes asked to leave. So off I went to find yet another daycare facility that would care for my baby. The time off work was getting tight and my boss was getting impatient.

She couldn't separate herself from me for one second. Leaving her to go to work was getting harder and harder.

I continued to do all that I had to do so that a court date could be required and so that I would be able to plead my case to the best of my ability. Therapists as well as the division of youth and family services were lining up to testify on our behalf. Everything was moving forward, and then finally, the final court date letter arrived in the mail. Basically, it stated: "Show up at 9am on this date and we will hand down our decision on this matter".

136

Journal Entry Twenty-Six

Decisions

Everyone showed up as requested. The judge approached the bench as he was announced and we remained standing until he sat. The buzz of the courtroom audience was reduced to a murmur and you could hear a pin drop. Everyone's jaw clenched tight waiting for him to speak.

He informed us that he had reviewed all of the reports, parent evaluations, statements, and hospital records and had made a decision. After careful consideration he made a decision to cease private visitation and switch to supervised visitation for Rojer until he ruled otherwise. I would bring the child to a neutral location for him to spend time with Destiny every other weekend and one day during the week.

I'm assuming Rojer was not happy with that decision. It was the last time we ever heard from or saw him again. Although the child support money still comes out of his paycheck every other week.

I guess we may never know what happened in the privacy on his 1-bedroom apartment with Destiny and even his other kids.

Destiny remained in therapy and life went on.

Decision #2. I'm sick of this house, sick of the memories, sick of everything. I want out of this house to move on with a new life with me and Destiny. I put the house up for sale and prayed for a miracle.

Decision #3. I'm sick of my current job. I need to find a way to make more money teaching, training, writing training materials, and more. So I jumped back into my own business with full force and began teaching at the local technical schools full-time. I was going to make this single mom life work dammit.

Decision #4. No more losers from the Internet! I'm sticking to my soul mate checklist and that was that! They had to have a full-time job, not live with their mama, have a car, and be <u>normal</u>. Is that too much to ask people!?

Journal Entry Twenty-Seven

Sad News

My Aunt was found lying on the floor in a state of confusion, unkempt, and barely breathing. She hadn't eaten or bathed for a week and the house was cluttered with everything from food wrappers to soda cans. The smell of garbage, urine and feces crowded the air and made it difficult for my Aunt Maryanne and my mother Rosalie to breathe as they made their way through the house trying to make sense of the chaos. The ambulance was on their way and they waited patiently with Aunt Terri, anxiously trying to get her to make sense of everything. But she was completely incoherent.

They say over the past weeks prior to the incident she was quiet, withdrawn, and sluggish. But they just thought she was tired. Her son Lorenzo was quite a handful with the drug use and his mental state.

The ambulance rushed her to the hospital. The phone call came from my mom. They thought she had a leaky heart, was the first diagnosis from the hospital. My mom said she thought it was because she smoked and was on birth control pills simultaneously for over 30 years. I wasn't familiar with that medical fact, but I'm sure my pill pack says not to smoke while taking them. Anyway, I was told to stay away for now. Her and my Aunt Maryanne had everything under control. I told her to keep me posted.

One of my cousins was also a nurse at the same hospital. Here is what was described to me:

Several doctors and nurses working frantically over my aunt. Emergency heart surgery. Cardiac Arrest. My mom and aunt in a state of disbelief and panic. Flat line...Code Blue!Clear!...Again!...Again!...flat line. Time of death 5:52pm. You can't give up, nooooo!Again, Clear!...3 minutes pass...Clear!...six minutes pass...beep beep beep...She's back!...It's a miracle!!! My mom and aunt breathe and whisper a silent prayer to God for saving their sister. Only one problem, six minutes deceased leaves a possibility of brain damage and/or memory loss. What a price to pay for a life.

I got another call from my mom. They brought her back after 6 minutes and she is alive. It was truly a miracle. I wonder if she saw the light. Or if there is a light. Maybe there is no light and just gates. No matter, she's back.

Heart surgery to attempt to repair the leaky heart would have to wait until she was stronger. I was able to visit a couple of days.

Aunt Terri was there, but not really there. The blank stare extended past me, the television screen, and out into the hallway. Every afternoon up until the surgery, I held her hand, kissed her cheek and sat with her while I read my book.

We thought the surgery was a success, but once again she went into heart failure. There was nothing more the surgeons, or doctors, or hospitals could do. She was way too weak. She was alive though, at least we had that. They would move her to a nursing home and keep her 'comfortable'. Not sure what that means either. Is that the medical term for drugged up? Either way it sounds very depressing.

Aunt Terri was my favorite. Always happy and laughing. The one who understood my constant plight against the naysayers who constantly asked me why I was always smiling and what did I have to be so damn happy about. She was the best listener, never judged, nothing but straight objectivity. She was the one I cried and laughed with through the good and bad times. And she had the most stress on her compared to my teeny weeny problems.

She had Niecy to care for, although Aunt Maryanne was happy to step in and care for her as always. She also had Lorenzo driving her nuts with his gang and drug dealer friends running through her house, he refusing to take his medication to keep his thoughts straight, and his drug paraphernalia all over the house. It was enough to make anyone explode. But she never did. She never got angry, never said a cross word about anyone, and always saw the good in everyone. I see that trait in my mom and Aunt Maryanne, and even in myself.

So they moved her into the nursing home. My cousin, who was a nurse came in the beginning and bathed her and kept an eye on her. I came a few days per week and spent the day helping her with her wig and putting on her toiletries and lipstick. She always had to look presentable for visitors. Although her speech was slurred, her memory was about 85% there. She knew who Destiny and I were and she was still laughing and cracking jokes. Her laugh was so infectious.

If I was not reading while she napped, I was being forced to watch movie re-runs on her favorite network, the Lifetime for women network. And then at meal time I would wheel her to the cafeteria and while she ate, we listened to the local piano entertainment. "Oh joy". It was enjoyable for her and it made her smile. That's all that mattered.

If the weather was nice I would wheel her to the sun-room or the outside courtyard for a little sunshine. I really tried to spend as much time as I could with her.

Then the call came. It was late Sunday afternoon. The sun was shining and it had just rained, so there were numerous prism colors decorating the sky. A single tear rolled down my cheek, followed by about a thousand more. There were not enough tissues in the world to dry my pain. She was gone and with the Lord and yet I was almost jealous. Now He would hear her laughter and jokes and not me. He would receive her brilliant smiles and not me. Not us. Everyone in the family would miss her dearly.

Lorenzo was nowhere to be found when the news came in. Some say he was living on the streets of New York City, and some say he was locked away in prison. It would be years before he would even hear the news.

Journal Entry Twenty-Eight

Second Chances

It was me and Destiny against the world. I was ready to pick myself up, stop feeling sorry for myself, and venture out into life again.

On this fine day, I was on my own. Taking a drive North for a networking event. They say the more people you meet the more likely you are to make a valuable connection. So I went.

After a grueling 2 hours of passing out business cards and shaking hands, I reapplied my sanitizing gel for the 10th time that day and stepped out into the fresh Fall air. While I was in the area I stopped at a few stores that carried my favorite hair supplies for natural hairstyles.

I was gazing into a window of a popular art gallery, a bit lost in my thoughts, when a voice from behind me utters "A true work of art." After coming out of my trance and turned ever so slightly over my right shoulder, my eyes focused on this tall, lanky guy with dregs. Kind of handsome and suave in his own way…and definitely charming.

"Oh no, I'm sorry, I wasn't coming onto you or anything", he says, "I was just admiring the same piece you were". (Yeah right. That's what they all say.) But you have to admit the line was good. There was softness, a gentle kindness, about him that was rare to see nowadays.

We shook hands and introduced ourselves and I gave him a card. (Always networking.) He asked if he could walk with me and I accepted.

Three hours later in a small coffee shop in a nearby village, we said good bye. I've never spoken with any man I just met about so many topics before, for so long, in my life! It was cozy and refreshing, and inspiring!

God had sent me a gem. A second chance at happiness. It was a perfect day. Until that night.

A mixture of fear and elation took over my emotions as I hung up the phone that night. A heart transplant donor had come in for my brother Darrell. A tragic car accident, the result of teenagers driving home drunk from a party, resulted in a new lease on life for my brother.

In twenty-four hours the heart of a teenager would be beating in his 48-year-old body. A miracle indeed.

Two days later Darrell is recovering at the University of Pennsylvania with his new heart. During his stay waiting for his new heart almost every one of his friends in the 'waiting ward' had passed on. And those that did not, received a new heart, and rejected it weeks or monthly later. It was a happy, yet quite scary, time for him, and me, and the rest of the family.

As I stood over his bed amazed at how he was sitting up, talking and laughing, I was more amazed at the staples going down the center of his entire chest and stomach.

I was also there when his doctor was reviewing the 30 or so anti-rejection and other medications he would be forced to take for the rest of his life.

I was sure this was the turning point my brother needed to turn his life around. No more drinking, smoking, drugs, or loose women. Ha! Maybe not the loose women part.

Journal Entry Twenty-Nine

The Book of Jeremy

Jeremy was the name of my second chance. I could write about him from cover to cover. That's how well we were getting to know each other. We liked the same books, music, foods, and places. Had the same hopes and dreams in life...you know the house and white picket fence. Except our dreams were more of a mansion with tennis courts and a pool.

Anyway, we started talking on the phone every day for hours and seeing each other several times per week. Turns out Jeremy met also 90% of my criteria checklist. He ran his own inventory company, had his own house that he inherited from his parents, his own car, and an average income. He was also honest, and funny, and had a great sexual appetite. Hooo-Ahh!

After a month or so I introduced him to my daughter, then 3 ½ at the time and they hit it off as well. She pronounced his name like (Jemmee), so Jem became my nickname for him.

I've never met an outdoors type guy so it was something for me to get used to. I don't like bugs and I don't like woods with bugs. Jem would have us out in parks, hiking, bikeriding, nature walks, and picnics. I sprayed Destiny and me with gallons of bug spray and packed our favorite snacks and we were off. The plus is that I was in the best shape ever. Gotta love those muscular calves on a woman, right?

We had done the family-thing… birthdays, weddings, retirement parties, etc... and everyone liked everyone. He was a handsome catch and exactly what I knew I deserved, Hell, I was a pretty good catch and exactly what he deserved as well, yadda yadda yadda.

But what did we think of each other? Well, to be honest when we looked into each other's eyes we saw nothing but love. Plain and simple. We both knew that we had found our soul mate.

One day while dining at one of our favorite restaurants he tells me to close my eyes and open my hand. I knew it damn well could not be a ring so I closed my eyes and hoped for the best. Destiny was all wide-eyed and anxious as well. She was already doing her Go-Mommy dance in her booster seat.

He placed something cold and flat in my palm and told me to open my eyes. I sat in silence and disbelief when I opened my eyes. Who knew a hunk of metal could make a girl cry? Of course I'm over-emotional and cry over everything, but that's not the point. Anyway, the object of my desire was a key. After only six months Jem was asking me to move into his house with them. He wanted us to live together as a family.

I was thrilled of course. Looking for a new way to renew myself and start over in a new place. It was the perfect opportunity. Although my parents would be disappointed because I was taking Destiny far away from them, but I also knew that they would understand. And they could still see her on the weekends. Especially if Jem and I wanted to have some alone time. I'm sure they would happily help a sista out…wouldn't they?

Well, here we are a month later standing in front of our new home with the moving truck. All his friends and family, including his brother, came over to help us (me and Destiny) move in. There were three bedrooms, one for his office, two bathrooms, a garage, driveway, and small fenced-in yard.

We were ready to begin our journey. The next level of our relationship.

I just heard from my mom, whom I hadn't heard from in several days. We usually spoke every day and I missed that. We begin talking and I can't believe the stuff she is telling me about my brother. I mean, we are all happy that he has not rejected the heart and has his youthfulness and energy back, but he is beginning to take it to the extreme and it has only been a year. Damn him! Haven't our parents had enough grief with the loss of one son? Parents are NOT supposed to bury their children!

Darrell was sneaking beer, smoking cigarettes and even a little weed, and God knows what else. What is wrong with him?! A second chance on life and this is what he does with it. After all of his buddies died right in front of him. After his own brother died from that 'life'.

My parents are beyond consoling. Their only recourse is to pray for him.

A few months later, I was cuddling in bed with Jem on a Sunday morning when the phone rang. My parents are rushing Darrell to the hospital. But it is not what you think.

Apparently, the loose women part <u>didn't</u> go away, even though the doctor told him he was not healthy enough for heavy stimulation. So what does Darrell do? Darrell, the one on the 30 different medications for his heart.

He takes the blue pill.

Yes, I said it. The blue pill. Not only is it lethal to combine with his medications and for his heart, but the side effect is worse. IT WOULD NOT STOP WORKING.

After 12 hours he was admitted into the hospital in excruciating pain. As soon as you walk into the hospital room it was the center of attention, no pun intended. My mother immediately dropped to the floor. Nurses and doctors ran in to pick her up off the floor and place her on the stretcher. I would have fainted too but I couldn't stop staring. Holy cow! That's not even human. I'm assuming the loose woman was walking around with a great big smile and smoking a cig right about now.

After the chaos, my mom and I left this visit to my Dad, and left the hospital. Since she came with my dad, I drove her home in my car to lie down.

Anyway, after over 24 hours they had no other recourse but to drain it. With a VERY LONG needle.

More excruciating pain for Darrell. I'm really hoping he learned his lesson this time.

And so life goes on.

Journal Entry Thirty

Keeping the Romance Alive

I must admit to you, there were some pros and cons about living in the home Jem grew up in. Childhood friends and girlfriends to sum it up. He had one of those cool sets of parents that everyone was jealous of. Stop by anytime for good conversation and a home cooked meal! Or better yet, a board game or game of Spades. Ugh!

Well apparently everyone in the neighborhood grew up and those rules still applied. There were literally people stopping by from the am to the pm, and all hours of the night. I met a new friend of Jem's every day. Not that they were not nice, or that the conversation was not tantalizing and intriguing, but enough was enough.

One time Jem and I had this romantic evening planned with dinner and candles and our bodies close together, and just as I was reaching ecstasy on the downstairs couch, which was by the front door mind you, someone stops by, knocking on the door as if they didn't get in, it would be the end of the world. I wanted to scream, and not in a good way…not the way I was hoping to. The problem is Jem is too nice of a guy to yell, "I'm busy, come back later!" He has to open the door, explain, talk some more, make excuses, and then close the door. Did I mention I wanted to scream?

This type of interruption happened a lot. Especially if it was an odd time of day and not nighttime, when we usually made love.

I remember one time when one of his friends was going through something with his wife and wanted to get away from her and the kids, so he came over out of nowhere. Now on this particular Saturday night Jem and I had my parents watching the baby and had to pick her up that night, so time was limited and *a wastin'*.

We thought he was going to stop by, say hi, see that we were in the middle of something, or about to start (ha!), and go back home. Instead, he sits right on the couch in between the two of us and starts getting into the movie that was on. Jem and I just looked at each other in disbelief. How could we get rid of him in a nice way? How long was he planning on staying?

About forty-five minutes go by and he is still there. Laughing at the movie and staring intently at the screen. He mentions he is hungry and says he is going to order Chinese and talk to us later. He finally left to pick up his food and he could not get out of the house fast enough.

Jem and I jump back on the couch, start ripping each other's clothes off and got to it. Twenty minutes later we were just about to have an orgasmic experience at the same time while in the 'canine' position when there was a knock at the door. I threatened to cut off Jem's gems if he stopped. He yelled, "Just a minute!" and we finished up. I scrambled for my clothes and ran into the bathroom. Jem pulled on his jeans and opened the door.

It was his friend again with the Chinese food he just picked up. He was going to eat it at our house instead of going home. UN-BE-LIEVE-ABLE!!

Anytime you are in a relationship for over a year it is important to spend alone time together and make an effort to keep the romance alive, you know? I try to be creative in all of my relationships. I'm a Scorpio, so that should explain a lot right there. Ha!

Lemme give you some examples. New Year's Eve, 2003. I set the stage in the kitchen with low lights and candles, soft music. I present my man with a color menu that I created on my computer with graphics and such outlining the schedule for the evening and the details of the appetizer, beverages, entree and dessert. Afterward I present him with a special art piece he had his eye on and then we made love. It was heavenly and I'll never forget those moments.

Next, Valentine's Day, 2004. We enjoy a lovely dinner at a local Spanish restaurant and come back home to exchange gifts. Again the music and candles set the mood. The music was always one of the special CD's that we would make for each other all the time. So onto my gift...since he is into Kama Sutra and has an exquisite book on this art of love, I decided to purchase this special game I found. It was a board game that tested your love with various Kama Sutra moves, including thoughtful, loving moves on each card such as telling your partner how they make you feel or how much you love them before giving them a kiss. Again, exquisite.

Okay, one more. I'm hoping I'm giving you some ideas you can use. Valentine's Day, 2005. We weren't supposed to hook up 'til Sunday and I was at my parents since Friday night. I give him a call

Saturday afternoon from an undisclosed location, (the hotel room I booked), and tell him to pack an overnight bag and come to this address. He was completely baffled and had no idea where he was going. I wanted to tell him to pack his swim trunks for the hot tub but I didn't want to give too much of the surprise away.

He arrived at the hotel and called my cell phone. I told him to take the elevator to the fifth floor and knock on room 515.

When he opened the door he was grinning from ear to ear! There were rose pedals on the floor and the bed, red Valentine's Day balloons everywhere, and me standing there looking gorgeous in a 2-piece red lace number and stilettos. You can figure out how the rest of the weekend went, right?

I'd like to share with you a poem that I wrote for him. It means so much to me that I can share this with you. It's in that new form of poetry called the *spoken word*. Just imagine a sassy black woman reading it aloud to an audience. Okay, here goes:

Your Swagga

Who do you think you are? Standing with yo' feet planted firmly on the ground, with your arms crossed, lookin' all confident an' shit

Yo' dregs blowing in the wind like palm trees on a warm summer day

I knew you had swagga but did you think you could fool me?

Underneath that intelligent, almost nerd-like, interior, is an exterior of an elephant

Tough and durable, guaranteed to stand the test of time

When you walk down the street you know you got it goin' on,

 that yo' shit don't stink

That your swagga was tight

Damn I almost lost sight...of what was most important

It's not all about the swagga and the way you make my toes curl and my knees shake every night

But the way you make my heart 'thump thump' when you look into my eyes and say those 3 little words

Yes, I said it, those 3 small words that all women long to hear, but that most men take for granted

I... love...you

There I said it!

Tingles shoot up my spine and the hairs on my arms stand to attention

Did somebody say my name? Am I the lucky next contestant on the "Love is Right"?

Shit, nobody told me I was next or I would've worn my new dress

This swagga can't be all mine, with a walk so fine

I knew I shoulda worn my new dress...damn.

Thinkin' bout the brown creaminess of your skin and the smoothness of it all melts my body like the summer sunshine

The same sun that alters your brown hair to reddish brown every single summer

The curve of your spine and hips reminds me of a mountainy road in sunny California

I imagine myself driving around the curves and slowin' down to admire the lovely scenery

Lovely and long are the road and the scenery, if you get my drift sista's

More than enough to satisfy my ample breasts, hips and thighs

I am mesmerized...by your swagga.

So those are just some of the ways that we kept the romance in our relationship. Not that we did not fight once in a while, but for the most part, life was good.

Until the phone call...

Journal Entry Thirty-One

Deja Vu

The rain was poundin' on my window like it was mad at somebody. And it was dark enough to confuse the morning with the night. The best kind of sleepin' weather in my opinion. So who the hell was calling me at 6am in the damn morning? Damn!

I reached for the phone and checked the caller ID. It was my mother. I could barely understand her. She wasn't making any sense. Something about Darrell and a phone call in the middle of the night from the hospital. My dad took over after a minute and explained.

You see, yesterday Darrell went into the hospital for a routine checkup of his new heart, which he does every 6 months. Nothing special. My mom and dad saw him after his tests at the hospital and said good night and told him they would pick him up the next day. He was sitting up laughing and smiling. The nurses were all smiles and talking about what a miracle it had been that he was going on his 11th year with his new heart and no problems! You see, all the nurses loved my brother. He was quite charming when he wanted to be.

Little did my parents know that it was the last time they would say good night to their son. At 1am the hospital nurse called to inform my parents that Darrell had passed. His new heart had finally given out. They tried to resuscitate him but to no avail.

My mother thought it was a wrong number. She could not understand what the crying nurse was babbling about. She yelled, "What do you mean he's gone?!! We just saw him this evening and he was fine!"

My mother did not want to wake me and needed time to collect her thoughts, so she waited until morning to call. Another tragedy. Another son lost. Another brother gone. How could life be so good and so cruel at the same damn time?

I hung up the phone and got on the road. I needed to be with my family so I drove to them as fast as I could. Jem would come join me later. He tried to console me but I could not speak. My mind was a blank as I drove down the turnpike lost in memories of my brother and the talks we had in life...about life.

He was a husband (although separated from his wife), a son, a father, and a brother, and a friend.

The immediate family had already gathered when I arrived. His estranged wife and his daughter (my niece) had been notified. Entenmann's containers were scattered across the kitchen table and the smell of coffee attacked my senses as I walked in the door. I was grabbed by Isaiah Jr. and my dad, and then my mother. The tears ran like the rain falling from the sky; steady and heavy. Hadn't I been here before? *Deja Vu.*

I don't want to depress you with the next couple of days but basically my parents were non-existent mentally, and understandably so. I took care of all of the arrangements, my aunt handled the memorial arrangements at our home church, and I wrote out all the notices by hand and mailed them off.

In addition, my god-sister, Sonya, traveled up for the memorial and together we planned the gathering at my parents' house for after the service. We made sure there were enough food and drink and desserts for the entire family. Over 60 people showed up to pay their respects. Relatives traveled from miles and miles away, some traveled across multiple states. It was so nice to see everyone and spend time with them, even under the circumstances. You have to understand that some I hadn't seen in years…decades even.

Once every couple of hours you would see my mom, dad or even me, sneak into the back of the house for a moment of silence and shed more tears. We were all trying to be strong for each other. I just kept thinking to myself that I was a little girl with three brothers not so long ago. Now I was a grown woman and down to one last living sibling, my brother Pookie. What went wrong? Was there something I could have done? I know that my parents had done everything they could to help, even pay for cars, educations, homes, vacations, and even rehab programs, but to no avail. I couldn't have done any more than that for sure.

So we picked ourselves up and put on our half-smile and ventured back out into the front of the house to greet and mingle with guests.

I was wondering something. Let me know what you think. Does it matter if someone is dying for a long time and then pass, or if they pass suddenly with no cause...does it hurt any more or less? I think it hurts just the same. When my first brother passed every day he was dying a little more and it was like ripping a piece of my heart out each day. But when

Darrell passed suddenly it was like the shock and unexpectedness of it ripped my entire heart out immediately and not gradually. What the hell is the difference?

So life goes on. Jem was there with the family and everyone was cooing over Destiny and how she's grown, and afterward we all go back to our mundane lives. But we never really forget; we just cope. And I truly believe a parent never really moves on after the death of one child, let alone two. They just cope in order to survive. My parents have never been the same since.

Journal Entry Thirty-Two

Let's Talk About Sex!

What is it about sex that intrigues us 'humans' so? Is it the need to release the stress of life? Is it to please our mate? Or is it to conform to the protocol of our 'species'? Some of us have an innate primal need to connect with our 'mates'. Thinking that if we do so it will bring us so close that we can read their innermost thoughts. Seeing through them if you will.

I would never have sex just to please my mate or to follow protocol or pro-create. I'm more of a sensual, romantic soul. I do try to become as one with my mate to get to know them on another level. Not that it means I can tell when they are lying, 'cause it doesn't. Ha!

A healthy sex life is important in any relationship. You should be able to express your inner most feelings and share any fantasies with your significant other. Trying new things in new places will keep the relationship alive and fresh. So in other words, Jem and I were not missionary style, in the bed, at 9pm, Monday through Friday, type lovers.

Not that we were public places type people, but we did keep it interesting in different parts of the house, and occasionally the back seat of his SUV.

Our lovemaking usually occurred in phases, and almost like an art, if you ask me. We began with the eye contact. You know, that look that lets you know the other person is 'feening' and ready? Ha!

Then we move to phase two, kissing. Long passionate kisses that go on forever and usually end up requiring a change of panties on my part.

Then phase three, the undressing. Unbutton this, unlatch that, unhook this, and rip that the hell off!

Next, onto phase four. And some of you I apologize may not be familiar with this term. It is called f-o-r-e-p-l-a-y. You may need to look that up. I'll wait while you get a dictionary. It is a form of touching body parts slowly and softly to stimulate arousal in your mate. You can be standing up, sitting, or lying down. Notice I said slowly and softly. That's because there are some grunts out there who think slapping and squeezing and the like, are foreplay. They are not. And should be reserved for actors and actresses in porno movies. Period.

So we are all worked up after 30 minutes and ready for the mind-blowing phase…Sex. While still kissing we begin the act in the selected position and his contorted faces tell me that my daily Kegel exercises are paying off and he is more than gratified. As we move to the sounds of Alicia Keys, Phyllis Hyman, and Sade, I'm thinking how much I love this man. Our movements remind me of the rhythmic rowing of a boat. Like I used to do in summer camp. Strenuous yes, but so worth when you reach the other side of the lake. Ha!

Jem can no longer hold on and he is about to explode. He wraps his arms around me and squeezes tight and releases the tensions of the day. After he releases he is surprisingly still ready to play and I began my stride to the finish, sprinting faster and faster until the moment when I win the race and crowd applaudes! "Aaaaaaaaaa!" I scream, "Yes, Yes, Yes, I did it!" and slump over in exhaustion.

And then we slept.

Journal Entry Thirty-Three

Self-Analysis

Life is like a box of chocolates. You know the rest. I've been dealt quite a few different blows in this life so far. From loves lost to tragic deaths. Molestation to attempted rape. Personal Accomplishments and Romantic Encounters. And of course the birth of my most precious gift, Destiny.

I decided to take all of this that was dealt to me and not let it destroy me. I kept a smile on my face in public, all the while dropping to my knees in prayer and crying in private; yet I held my head up high. No one could steal my joy. This was one of the valuable lessons I learned from the long talks with my father. And believe it or not his most valuable speeches came out when he was high on alcohol.

My dad taught me to never let the 'man' (he's a bit 'ole school') see you sweat. Always persevere and never give up or quit. Fight for what you want out of life and most importantly...there are <u>no</u> shortcuts to the top...just hard work and perseverance.

I took our little talks to heart and applied them to my life as I made my way through undergraduate and graduate studies, corporate positions to sole proprietor of my own company, and from being a wife to a mother and eventually a single parent.

Although I must say it hurt when family members and certain friends in school treated me differently, laughed at me, or did not support me. I got used to being a loner after a while. I had to learn not to be ashamed of being attractive, or having hazel eyes and long hair, or dressing nice. I learned to be proud and live each day to the fullest.

I think this journal has been a major help in this regard. And sharing it with you has certainly been a turning point. My inner most feelings and deepest, darkest secrets, that even much of my family didn't know...revealed to a total stranger. Like coming out of the closet, you don't quite know what to expect. Will people shun you, hug you, or will you make them feel uncomfortable. You just never know.

But one thing's for sure, the experience is like a mental *colon cleansing*. Ha! Flush out the bad memories of the past and negative thoughts and refresh your mind with the present and future...positive thoughts only.

So what's the deal with Jem? And why so many problems with the men in my life? Those from the past and present. I think girls at a young age always look up to their fathers; at least it was for me. I was totally spoiled by my dad and pretty much got everything I wanted in life growing up, and even now. It's a form of unconditional love that cannot be explained. As I mentioned previously my hugs and kisses came mostly from my dad and not my mom. Not that she was cold but just more conservative and reserved. But she loved me just the same. She showed it in her own way.

Anyway, as an adult I somehow wanted the man of my dreams to treat me like my dad, holding expectations way too high. In this day and age you could barely get a man to pay for your value meal at McD's.

Chivalry is pretty much dead except for in a few men. Very rarely does a man hold the door open for you, pay for your meal or embrace your child or children.

So what is the end result? Bottom line. Even if I did not have Jem I would be focusing on my business, taking care of my little one, and have my own crib. That pretty much sums it up.

Journal Entry Thirty-Four

Happily, Ever After?

Why is it that every man hates the following three words? "Can we talk?" All I said was "Can we talk?" and Jem was running for the door, saying that he needed something urgent from the local Home store and had to go.

I knew this day would come one day. Things were going so well. Too well. It had been five years and I was still living with Jem "in sin" as my mother would say. I had to bring up the "where is this relationship going" question. I just had to.

Jem walks in with a handful of bags from the store, probably about to redo the hardwood floors for the eighth time or re-do the entire kitchen for all I know. I stopped him before he got started and sat him down on the couch. Destiny was quietly watching her favorite DVD in her room upstairs.

I said to Jem that I was happy, loved our life and wanted to know if he was ready to take our relationship to the next level. But it seems he was happy with the way things were and was not in a position to purchase a ring, and pay for a wedding. The house needed a lot more work and he was doing all the repairs and upgrades himself.

So what do I do? As I said before I could take care of myself and Destiny on my own with no problem, with my income from my company, but what is success without the one you love. It's like that Alicia Keys song "Doesn't Mean Anything".

Ultimatums never work either.

So I offered a middle ground. I wanted to work towards saving our money together and get engaged by the end of the year, another seven months from now. If we could not make it work at that point, Destiny and I would move out and onward.

I was just about to get up from the couch when the phone rang. It was the doctor's office with my test results from the blood work I had done the previous week when I had a bout of the flu. I was listening intently to what he was saying while trying to ignore Jem breathing down the back of my neck. Uh huh...yes... I understand... okay... um... well... okay...thank you Dr. Reed.

I didn't understand that entire conversation. I hung up the phone dazed and confused; my jaw hanging slightly open. I turned around to confront Jem about the results and had to lower my head to meet his gaze. Somehow, he knew. He was on his knees grinning from ear to ear. The next three words that came out his mouth resulted in a flow of tears and roar of laughter at the same time.

Jem asked, "Can we talk?"

A month later we were engaged and set a date for after the birth of Destiny's brother, Paris. Jem was moving his office downstairs and the office upstairs would be the nursery. Life was good.

It was just like my dad had said, I kept my head up and didn't give up and sure enough there was a light at the end of tunnel. I look back at my life…the pains, the joys, the ups and downs, the laughter and the loss. And I know at any given time I could have crumbled…simply gave up…but I didn't, I persevered. I went from a black child to a black woman and I survived.

About the Author

 *Cheryl Powell,* (writing under pen name Cheryl Denise Bannerman), is a multi-genre author of three successful works of fiction, a motivational speaker, and CEO. She resides in Orlando, Florida, where she runs a virtual Training and Development company, GC Learning Services LLC dba Learn2Engage, which she founded in 1996.

"My mother introduced me to books at an early age and encouraged me to not only read but also write. I remember having my first poem published in a collective book of poetry at the age of only 13. And when my mother wasn't working, I would read her my short stories, soaking in her edits and feedback like a sponge. Even at an early age, I was searching for perfection in my writings."

Through the trials and tribulations of her life, she has learned to heal through her writing. One of the few female authors to introduce topics of social concern within 'fictional' stories, her books draw from the most intimate life experiences and include characters who have been victims of child molestation and domestic violence, and who suffer from depression and various other addictions. For example, her second book, Words Never Spoken, which just won the 2018 Book Excellence Award, is a self-help, poetry, chapter-book about a woman who escaped an abusive relationship, and even includes self-reflection journal pages for readers to document their feelings and begin healing.

Her goal in life is to keep writing and continue helping victims of Domestic Abuse/Violence, Grief and ANON family groups, and Corporate Health and Wellness groups, to heal through words — encouraging them to 'write the pain' via journaling, and expressing themselves through short stories, songs, and poetry.

What Did You Think of Black Child to Black Woman?

First of all, thank you for purchasing this book, Black Child to Black Woman. I know you could have picked any number of books to read, but you picked this book, and for that, I am <u>extremely grateful</u>.

I hope that it added value and quality to your everyday life. If so, it would be awesome if you could share this book with your friends and family by posting to social media.

If you enjoyed this book and found some benefit in reading this, I would like to hear from you and hope that you could take some time to post an online review. Your feedback and support will help me to greatly improve my writing craft for future projects and make this book even better.

Visit the web site at www.bannermanbooks.com for contact information.

I want you, the reader, to know that your opinion is very important to me and hope that you will check out my other works of fiction:

Title	*Category/Genre*
Words Never Spoken	*Women's Inspirational/Poetry*
A Killer's Reflection	*Erotic Psychological Thriller*
Cats, Cannolis and a Curious Kidnapping	*Book 1: Cozy Mystery Series*
A Bloody Stiletto, Cold Lasagna, and a Bestseller	*Book 2: Cozy Mystery Series*

Cheryl Denise Bannerman